The Maid Of A Princess

Volume 1

Sage Guarino
2021. Vol. 1 1st Edition
Copyright © 2021 Sage Guarino.

ISBN: 979-8416487539

Any refrences to historical events, real people, or real places
are used fictitiously. Names, characters, and places are prod-
ucts of the author's imagination

Story written by Sage Guarino.

Cover art done by Kapi Workshop/Sage Guarino.

Interior images done by Kapi Workshop/Sage Guarino.

Rear Cover art done by Kapi Workshop/Sage Guarino.

First Edition 2021 Vol. 1

E-mail: Sagesnovels@gmail.com

volume 1
Contents
THE MAID OF A PRINCESS

Prologue

The warm air of the forest embraced my lungs with open arms as I darted through the vast unknown. I had stolen the princess's most valued possession, and now I was on the run. Arrows of all types penetrated the leafy world around me, but I was untouchable.

Unlike the other demihumans of this world, I, Keiko Hiro, am able to wield even the most powerful magic known to man.

The sounds of a dozen men on horseback chasing me through the forest brought joy to my dry, empty soul. I couldn't help but laugh; the excitement of being on the chase brought tears of joy to this poor orphan's face. You see, even though my name stood for 'lucky child,' I was anything but fortunate. My mother had been disgusted to have given birth to a demihuman.

In the land of Geatree, to give birth to a demihuman was considered a curse from the gods, a judgment for committing some sort of sin; hence there were few demihumans around.

When I was born, Mother simply tossed me away into the world, leaving me to die. I was found by an old man who went by the name of Mist. He took me in and raised me till the age of seventeen. I considered him to be my grandfather. I learned the

skill of thieving from him. From pickpocketing to bank robberies, we did it all to survive, until one day, when he was caught
by the royal guards and thrown into the dungeon. After his trial,
he was given a five-year sentence. Our plan was to wait until
he was released to attempt our biggest heist yet: the theft of the
princess's amethyst necklace, but that didn't pan out.

King Bowatani, ruler of the Zaria Kingdom, was unhappy with
Grandpa's sentence. In the end, the king had him beheaded in
front of the whole kingdom, humiliating him.

I swore to myself on that day that I would steal the princess's
necklace and complete the heist, not just for Grandpa's sake, but
for the both of us. And that's how I ended up here, in the forest,
being chased by the royal guards.

Up ahead of me, about one hundred feet away was a large
gorge stretching fifty feet in width. Unlike the guards, I was capable of using jumping magic.

As adrenaline rushed through my veins, my eyes widened with
excitement at the thought of the jump. I pointed my wolf-like ears
backwards to achieve the best aerodynamic figure that I possibly
could. With every step closer to the gorge, my heart pounded

more heavily. The light shining through the trees exposed my eyes to the other side. With every ounce of might and magic in my body, I jumped.

Time slowed down. I looked back over my shoulder, only to see thirty arrow shafts following my journey to the other side. I whispered the word *tempest* into my palm, then with a closed fist, I placed my hand on my lips and blew all the air from my lungs into the center of my fingers.

In the blink of an eye, every arrow began to change direction, spinning in a circle as if blown by a tornado. The guards swerved away as all the arrows started to fling back towards them.

I was invincible, a god in disguise! That is, until I landed on the other side. A chuckle broke free from my lips. "See you later, losers!"

Ding!

And just like that… I blacked out.

When I woke, I found myself enclosed by a row of steel bars. I glanced to the left, then back to the right. *What in the world, where am I?* A smooth, alluring voice made its way into the tips of my ears.

"Oh good, you're awake." I glanced over, past the steel bars and towards the soft voice.

In front of me, a short, womanly figure was standing, one who happened to be wearing a large, clearly expensive sun hat. I was still dizzy from the sudden blackout and unable to see clearly. "Who are you, and why am I locked inside of this cage?" I asked.

"Look, I get it; I stole something valuable from the princess, but to be fair, you guys did leave it out in the open!"

"Silence!" the figure shouted.

My ears perked up in sudden shock. Within a few seconds, a sudden pain made itself present on the back of my head. "Ouch, what the heck?"

I reached behind my ears and placed my hand on the aching spot. The woman laughed.

"About that—it might have something to do with this." She brought her hand out from behind her back, exposing a frying pan.

"Wait, what?" I shouted. "You mean to tell me that you clubbed me with a frying pan?!"

She smiled, and the seal of her lips broke, revealing perfect white teeth. "Look, you seem like a nice girl, but I don't have time for this. Just take the necklace and return it to the princess so I can be on my way."

Her hand came up and brushed her long, thick golden hair back behind her ear. "Don't worry, the necklace has already been returned to the princess," she said.

I sat back in confusion. "What do you mean? You're the one holding the..."

And that's when it hit me. The princess had been in front of me the entire time. "...wait, you mean..."

"Mm-hmm. Yes, it is I, Princess Valentina."

I grabbed hold of the steel bars and directed my attention over to the butler, who had been watching from a distance. He was chuckling in my direction. Fear lanced through my body. *Was I about to fall victim to the kingdom and suffer the same fate as Grandpa? No, I shall not let someone else determine my fate!*

"Listen princess, I have somewhere to be, so can we get this over with? A buddy of mine said that there are some hot babes down at the local bar, so I'd like to go now." I put on my best smile, while doing my best to give off a hint of seduction with my eyes.

"Yeah, no," she answered.

I pointed my ears downwards and began to speak in a soft tone. "Please?" I asked.

But she ignored me.

She called over one of her servants and had him place the necklace around her neck. What happened next was something I'd thought only existed in fairytales. Little bright orbs of all colors surrounded her body. It was visible magic.

You see, in the land of Geatree, even though magic was known to exist, it was rare for it to be visible. Up until this point in my life I'd thought I was the only being in the kingdom who was able to wield visible magic.

If it wasn't for the little orbs highlighting her womanly figure, I might not have noticed. She was curvy from head to toe. Her baby blue eyes sparkled off her dress's bright purple fabric. The silver chain enhanced her neckline, and the amethyst crystals hung low towards her breasts. I started to drool, but I caught myself in time. *Forget the women at the bar ... this is where I need to be.*

The orbs disappeared one by one, and as they did, the princess removed her large hat and handed it to her butler.

"Do you know why I had you locked up in this cage?" she asked.

"Because I stole your necklace?" I replied, in my most sarcastic tone.

"No, silly. Well, yes ... but that's not all." I sat there confused. *What does she mean by that's not all?*

"I heard from my royal guards that you are capable of using visible magic. Is that true?"

"Yeah, I can use it," I said, while trying to figure out why she was asking me.

The sudden change in her body language told me that she was oddly happy at my answer, even though she didn't want to show it. "Good. As of today, you, Keiko Hiro—"

"Wait … how do you know my name?" I asked.

She chuckled. "I have my ways. As I was saying, as of today, you, Keiko Hiro, have now been assigned the role of personal royal maid."

Everyone in the room stopped what they were doing and directed their attention towards Princess Valentina. Glasses hit the floor as butlers and maids dropped their trays in shock.

"Princess! This is absurd!" one of the butlers shouted.

"This thief, as your personal maid? My lady, are you feeling alright?" asked one of the cooks.

"Enough!" she said. "As a gift for my seventeenth birthday, my father, *the King*, has said that I could have anything I wanted. And I want *him* to be my personal maid!"

Specks of spit were flung from my lips as I dropped to my knees and began to laugh. "Oh princess, you're really funny. Okay, the joke's over. Let me out now."

"I was being serious."

A moment of silence went by. I blinked twice. "What?" The sound of my shout could be heard echoing throughout the halls of the palace. The king came rushing in with his royal guards. "Is everything okay?" he asked.

"I will never do as you say!" I exclaimed.

The king walked towards me and opened the cage. He was a very short, muscular man with a large and curly mustache. Just looking at him made my blood boil. I wanted to kill him on the spot for what he'd done to Grandpa, but if I did that I knew the royal guards would kill me for sure.

Now's my chance to escape. As I began to leap out of the cage, he reached out his arm and grabbed me by the ear. "Guards, get the collar," he said. *Collar? What collar?*

Before I could comprehend the situation, the royal guards had placed a cold metal collar around my neck. The frozen texture of the metal sent shivers down my spine. "What the heck is th—"

"Quiet!" the king shouted.

"Jeez, okay I get it," I said, while slowly stepping backwards.

Princess Valentina placed a similar-looking bracelet around

her wrist and walked towards me. The guards grabbed my arms and held me still. *Why is she getting so close?* I wondered.

Within a few seconds, the princess's face was a mere inch from mine. Sweat rolled down my cheeks, and my heart began to pound. She smelled like lilies. *Is it some kind of perfume, or her natural scent?* I couldn't tell. She licked her lips, then looked me in the eyes. "Hey, do you want to tell me why you're so cl—"

Before I knew it, our lips were sealed together in an oddly romantic kiss. Her lips were soft, maybe even the softest I had ever felt. I could feel the warmth of her body entering mine through the cracks in her lip gloss.

After a few seconds, she finally released her hold on me. As my body began to heat up, I shouted, "What the heck was that?"

She giggled. The collar around my neck and the bracelet around her arm both began to glow blue.

"The contract has successfully been created," the king said. I stood there in utter confusion.

"You see, boy, these metal rings have my daughter's magic infused into them. Whomever she kisses whilst wearing those rings is bound to her soul. In other words, you are now officially my daughter's maid. If she asks anything of you, the collar around your neck will glow blue, just as it did now, and your body will complete the task commanded of you without hesitation."

"Wait a minute. Aren't maids normally female? And why choose me? You're probably better off just getting a woman to assist you," I said, laughing uneasily.

"Don't look at me—I wanted to kill you," the king said.

What…?

"It was my daughter who spared your life by making you her maid. You should be thankful."

She looked over at me. "Sit," she said.

Without hesitation, my body dropped to the floor.

"Waaah!" *What the heck is happening right now?*

I looked over towards the princess. Her face was turning red and she stood there quietly smiling.

And that is how I ended up becoming *The Maid of a Princess.*

Chapter 1
A Maid's Ranking

The princess was taking me down to the local tavern to register as an Adventurer.

I unwillingly made my way down towards the Adventurers' Guild as the princess had instructed. It wasn't as if I really had a choice; the collar around my neck made it impossible to leave her side.

Why did she choose me to be her personal maid? I wondered. *It's not like I'm all that special.*

"Do you want to tell me why I'm registering as an adventurer? I thought I was supposed to be your butler?"

"I think you mean my maid," said the princess.

I glanced off into the distance. "Whatever. Forget the title, what are we doing here and why are you wearing a cloak?"

She ignored my questions and motioned me inside the tavern. Once inside, she pointed to the front desk. *This is so stupid,* I thought.

As I made my way towards the front desk, I couldn't help but notice that the room had gone silent. I could feel the eyes of the tavern drawn to me in disgust.

Being a demihuman, I was used to such treatment. After all, we are considered to be bad luck, so it was nothing new. Eventually I made it to the desk, and sitting behind it was a short, red-eyed woman.

"Hello, welcome to the Adventurers' Guild. My name is Lola. How may I assist you today?"

"We would like to both sign up as adventurers, please," said the princess. I glanced over in her direction with a clear look of confusion on my face.

Both…? She's signing up too? I thought.

The tavern lady smiled with what I could only assume was joy.

"How wonderful," she said. "We've been short staffed when it comes to adventurers lately. They all keep dying."

"Excuse me?!" I shouted.

Grabbing my arm, the princess whispered in my ear. "Be quiet."

Dying from what? The goblins and the elves had both been defeated by the kingdom years ago, and since then no mythical creatures of greater power had been documented.

In the land of Geatree, mythical creatures such as the dragons, ogres, cyclops, and so on, are all beings of visible magic in its purest form—in the sense that they have been created by the goblins and the elves.

The goblins are considered to be the strongest magic users in all of Geatree, after the elves, who were eradicated centuries ago in the great war. The goblins managed to survive the great war by hiding in caves underground.

After the elves had been defeated, they decided to harness all of their spiritual energy by sacrificing their bodies to the king of all mythical beasts, the Great Dragon, Larx.

Once harnessed, they'd immediately gone into hiding and hadn't been seen since. Ever since that day, all of Zarias's problems with mythical beasts have vanished, ultimately leaving the Adventurers' Guild as a useless organization. Adventurers from all over the kingdom were forced to resign and find other means of living.

Every now and then, a smaller creature such as a slime or mega wolf would appear, but they are barely a threat. This lack of threat therefore made me curious as to why the few adventurers who still held their positions were being killed.

"Yes. We would love to sign up," the princess said.

Lola smiled. "Oh perfect, right this way."

She led us Into a nearly pitch dark room that had a single small light in the center. Once we entered, Lola made her exit and the door behind us slammed shut. *What in the world is happening?*

Shortly afterward, a scraggly voice could be heard from above: "Can you guys hear me okay?"

The princess seemed unfazed by the situation. She glanced up towards the ceiling. "Yeah, we can hear you loud and clear."

In the center of the room, under the light, sat what looked to be a statue carved from stone. Upon further inspection it was clear that it was a dwarf gargoyle. Its eyes seemed enraged and the spines on its back were standing up in anger.

After I asked why we were locked in this dark musty room, the voice began to explain how this would determine our adventurer rank.

According to the voice, the gargoyle had been imprisoned in stone hundreds of years ago by the elves. By placing our hands on the statue, all of the magic in our bodies would seep into the stone, causing it to undo the imprisonment.

The voice then explained how no living being had ever been able to fully undo the spell.

They therefore determined your ranking based on how much of the gargoyle you were able to release.

Non-magic users were subject to other means of ranking. By being magic users, we already had the foundation rank of "M" to build onto.

The ranking system was measured first through magic, then through physical skill and abilities. Non-magic users were capable of ranks "D" through "AAA", and magic users were capable of ranks "M-D" through "M-AAA". Normal non-magic users were incapable of reaching the M ranks, simply because they were unable to wield magic. The perks of being in the M ranks were better bounties and limited offers only available to those who held such a rank.

"Once the magic transfer has been completed, the gargoyle

should return to its statue-like state," said the voice.

So it is a real gargoyle. That explains why it looks so genuine.
I thought.

After a brief discussion with the princess, it was decided that I would go first.

Earlier, Lola had given the princess and me empty adventurer cards, which when activated would serve as our ID cards, as well as a means of checking our rankings.

I walked towards the gargoyle with a sense of pride and ease. *This is going to be a piece of cake!*

All I had to do was place my hand on the gargoyle, transfer some of my magic into that thick stone skull, and then be on my way with my "M-AAA" ranking. *With a ranking like that, who knows what endless bounties I'll be able to pursue.*

Although it occurred to me that there hadn't been many mythical beast sightings in the past few hundred years, so there probably weren't many high-paying bounties. *Eh, whatever.*

I slowly raised my hand, placing it carefully on the top of the gargoyle's bumpy head. The texture of the stone was rough, almost like that of sandpaper, and the feeling it gave me was one that shot shivers down the back of my neck. I shut my eyes and pointed my ears upwards in an attempt to achieve ultimate concentration. Within a few seconds I could feel all the magic in my body start to flow out through my hand and into the gargoyle. For a moment I felt at ease, like I was a heavenly river bestowing a blessing on the gargoyle. I opened my eyes briefly, only to see that my magic was illuminating the entire room.

Bits and pieces of stone started to fall off the gargoyle, exposing its thick, purple, leathery skin.

My eyes widened as the room got brighter. I looked over towards the princess, but again, she looked quite unfazed.

Bit by bit, the gargoyle started to break free from the stone shell that held it captive. It was a magical sight, one might even say it was holy. The stone around its face began to break off, allowing the creature to breathe. Its nose was small, and it had two abnormally large fangs in its lower jaw that covered most of its face. It was oddly adorable. I felt as if I had given birth to this creature, for the gargoyle and I were two souls united as one for a short, magical moment.

Eventually, the magic in my body began to drain dry, and as it did so the gargoyle began to once again convert back to its frozen state. For a creature who had looked so menacing in the stone, it truly was calm. *What a poor creature.* I thought. *Trapped away in this prison forever.*

Within a few moments of completing the magic transfer, I heard the scraggly voice once again: "Good job. I am honestly amazed! I've never seen anyone tame the gargoyle like that with their magic!"

I felt honored in that moment, like I was on top of the world.

The voice then explained that if I placed my right hand on the blank ID card, my adventurer rank would reveal itself.

I eagerly removed the card from the pocket of my leather jacket, and put my right hand over it. A small blue light illuminated the card from under my hand. Once the light had faded away, I was able to read the card. "Let's see ... let's see ... let's see!"

I flipped the card over and to my surprise I was—"Rank M-A! How is this even possible? You said I was the only one who had ever tamed the gargoyle using magic! I deserve a triple A ranking at least."

I was filled with anger as I stood there in confusion. *This is rigged.*

The voice merely laughed in an oddly cute yet scraggly tone. I looked back down at my ID. Under "Title" it read, "The one."

I was once again confused. *The one?*

"Alright. It's your turn now," said the voice.

I looked over at the princess, who was still hiding her face behind that cloak of hers. *There is no way she's going to beat my rank. I'm incomparable.*

She silently walked towards the gargoyle. When she reached it, she removed the hood of the old baggy cloak from her face and slammed her hand on top of the statue.

"Wait! Princess Valentina, is that you? You can't be in here!"

Within a matter of seconds, massive amounts of magic began to pour into the statue. Waves of pure energy shot out of the statue and into the room, some of which almost took my head off.

"Princess! What the heck is going on?" I shouted.

The room was so bright that I was unable to see; it was like staring into one of Geatree's three suns. I was blinded, but I was able to hear the door slam open. Lola had burst in, desperately trying to stop the princess.

"Princess, you have to take your hand off the—"

Boom!

The statue erupted, sending shock waves across the room. My head was starting to pound and I was thrown up against the wall. My vision had yet to come back, but my hearing was intact; I placed my hand on my forehead to help ease the pain of the blast. Loud unfamiliar screeches echoed throughout the room.

Eventually my eyesight came back, and when it did, I was greeted by an unexpected sight.

The princess had somehow managed to break the gargoyle free from the elves' imprisonment spell. I felt my chest tighten.

There's no way, I thought, but now was not the time to hesitate. A full-sized dwarf gargoyle was flying rampant around the room. I directed my attention to Lola, who was cowering in fear behind the princess. It was now or never; I had to save them.

I opened my palm and moved it towards my face.

"Tempest," I whispered.

Then, with a closed fist, I placed my hand on my lips and blew into the center of my palm. As I began to cast my spell, the princess was busy casting one of her own. With both her hands, she grabbed the amethyst stone on her necklace and shouted the words, "Electrica avem!"

A screech louder than the gargoyle's was instantly audible after her spell had been cast. The wind from my spell had been holding the gargoyle in place. *What the heck did she just cast? I don't see anyth—*

Before I could finish my train of thought, a black hole radiating visible magic opened on the side of the wall closest to the gargoyle.

Out of the hole a phoenix emerged, but not one made of fire, no; this one was crafted from the purest form of electrical magic that I had ever seen.

The ranking of electrical magic levels is done by color. The weakest being yellow, and the strongest being green, but this phoenix was a color unheard of for electrical magic. It was purple.

I couldn't help but be slightly scared at that moment. I feared the princess. *What does this mean? How powerful is she?*

The princess let off a loud scream, but not one of anger. This was one of control. She knew exactly what she was doing; the magic radiating off the phoenix glistened in her baby blue eyes.

Before I knew it, another magical blast occurred, causing a shock wave. I once again slammed into the wall.

Once I hit the floor, I immediately opened my eyes and placed my hands over my ears. All that was left of the room was rubble. To my right was Lola, and to my left was Valentina. The gargoyle and the phoenix were nowhere to be seen.

I looked over in the princess's direction while loudly coughing the dust out of my lungs. She was standing tall, without a single scratch on her. Her head was buried in her ID card. She had a confused look on her face. She turned to Lola. "Hey Lola. What does this mean?"

She flipped her ID over, exposing it to our eyes. It read:

"Name: Valentina Bowatani

Title: Elemental Purity

Status: Rank M-SSS"

"Triple S!" I shouted. "I didn't even know that was a ranking."

zvLola struggled to stand up. The expression on her face was clearly one of concern. Her eyes were watering. She was covered in debris from head to toe, but none of that seemed to matter to her. All she could do was focus on Valentina's ID. She whispered, "Triple S…"

Chapter 2
The Vault

After the explosion, and the revelation of the princess's rank, Lola swiftly moved the two new adventurers into a nearby room that had survived the magical blast.

What in the world just happened? I had never seen such powerful visible magic before. My body didn't know how to react; I was pouring with sweat and my hands were trembling in fear.

"Does somebody want to tell me what the heck is going on?" I shouted.

Lola, who looked just as concerned as I was, explained the situation. According to her, the princess had been forbidden to take the test to become an adventurer. A long time ago, her true magic had been sealed away for the sake of the kingdom's safety.

"You see, if the princess were to take the exam to become an adventurer, the seal on her magic would shatter, and her full abilities would slowly start to return to her. That is why the King forbade it, and I just committed the worst crime possible—I let her take the exam unknowingly!"

You mean to tell me that the power I just saw isn't her strongest spell?

Lola dropped to her knees and began to cry, tears filled her eyes and cheeks flushed blood red. I looked up at the princess, and it wasn't until that moment that she spoke. "It's true. Father placed a seal on my powers ages ago."

"Then why did you intentionally break the seal?" Lola asked hesitantly.

I bent down and put my arm around Lola. Then I took her hand and placed it on my head. If there was one thing I hated more than being the princess's maid, it was being pet like some kind of animal. It was humiliating, but at that moment I couldn't care less about my feelings. The look on Lola's face made me want to comfort her, no matter what.

I glanced at the princess. Her face was red and she seemed a bit flustered. *What's she so upset about?*

She then began to speak once again.

"I'm sorry to put you in this position, Lola. You can rest assured that my maid and I will not tell a single soul about what happened here today."

Wait just a second, this could be my way out of this slave col-

lar! All I have to do is tell the king about his daughter's actions and he will let me go in return for saving the kingdom from her powers! It's brilliant.

I smirked cockily. "You're done for now, princess! Wait until I tell the king that you..." *What the heck?*

"That I what?" she asked.

"That you..." *What is going on?*

"What the heck? Why can't I finish my sentence?"

It was then that it dawned on me that the princess had mentioned how we wouldn't tell a soul about what had happened. "You mean..."

The princess nodded in agreement. "Yes, because of the collar, you won't be able to tell a single person about the seal being shattered. So get that thought out of your head, Keiko. And while you're at it, brush the debris out of your hair, would you?"

My eyes widened as my mouth dropped open. *You have got to be kidding me.*

Lola looked up at the princess and once again asked her the

reason for committing her crime. Unwilling to expose her true intentions, Princess Valentina simply stated that it was for the greater good of the kingdom that her powers had been returned to her.

Lola once again broke down in tears. She stared at the princess whilst struggling to speak; her nose was runny and there was saliva coming from her mouth. I actually found her a tad disgusting at that moment. "But… but what about my building? This was my only source of income—without it I'm ruined."

The princess started to laugh. *What could possibly be so funny?*

"Oh, this little old place? Leave it to me."

The princess walked in my direction. I removed my arm from Lola's back and stood up. "What do you mean, leave it to you?" I asked.

"Don't worry about it," she answered.

Before I knew it, the princess had taken both her hands and placed them on my cheeks. Within seconds our lips were once again pressed together. *What the heck? She's kissing me, at a time like this?!* I refused to shut my eyes, instead staring at the princess in utter confusion. I glanced over towards Lola, who was looking in our direction.

"What are you two doing?" she asked. *I wish I knew myself.*

In a matter of seconds, an aura of yellow magic began to radiate off the princess. With our lips still sealed together, I felt my feet begin to lift from the ground.

"Mhhh!" I shouted. *What is happening?*

As we levitated higher, I glanced at my hands. My body, too, was emitting yellow magic. The princess opened her eyes, locking them with mine. It was at that moment I felt as if we had become one. The collar around my neck and the bracelet around her arm began to glow blue. I stared directly into her eyes. It was then that I could see it; the source of her magic was slowly releasing itself into her soul. The light on her bracelet began to glow even brighter, eventually getting so bright that I couldn't see anything beyond her beautiful eyes. What felt like an eternity passed by until she finally released my lips, and when she did, we fell to the floor.

I landed on my backside. "Ah, that hurt!"

When I looked up, the tavern had been completely restored, from the small crack in the window to the creaky floorboards. Even the bugs who had perished in the blast were back to their previous positions. I looked over towards Lola, and saw her scarlet eyes were shimmering in shock. I heard a voice not too far away.

"Ouch … I guess I didn't stick the landing."

It was the princess. She too had landed on her backside. "What in the world was that?" I shouted.

She looked up into my eyes. "Did you forget? With your collar and my necklace, we are now one soul combined. It was the power of both of our magic that restored the tavern."

The yellow aura around her body began to fade away, and as it did I couldn't help but wonder to myself, *Who is this woman?*

After we'd brushed ourselves off, the princess asked Lola to lead us to the vault.

This vault, unlike most, was not one that held money or jewels. No, the kingdom's vault was a place only the highest ranking adventurers were allowed to enter. There, they could discover the kingdom's top secret bounties and missions. Grandpa Mist and I had spent years searching for this place. Our hope had been to dig up some dirt on the kingdom and use it as blackmail, to gain riches.

Lola nodded her head. "Right this way, princess—you too, wolf boy."

"Seriously? Is that the thanks I get for doing my best to comfort you?"

Lola gestured with her hands and moved them in a circular motion. While doing so, she began to cast a spell in an unfamiliar language.

"⬚⬚⬚⬚ ⬚⬚⬚⬚⬚ ⬚⬚ ⬚⬚. ⬚⬚⬚⬚ ⬚⬚ ⬚ ⬚ ⬚⬚ ⬚⬚‖ ⬚ ⬚ ⬚ !¡⬚⬚⬚. ⬚⬚⬚⬚⬚ ⬚⬚⬚ ⬚⬚⬚ ⬚⬚⬚⬚ ⬚ ⬚ ⬚⬚⬚⬚ ⬚ ⬚ ⬚⬚⬚ ⬚⬚⬚⬚. ⬚!¡⬚⬚ ⬚ ⬚ ⬚⬚ ⬚⬚⬚ ⬚ ⬚ ⬚ ⬚ ⬚ ⬚ ⬚⬚ ⬚⬚⬚⬚⬚"

What in the world did she just say? In an instant, a black hole appeared between the palms of her hands. Slowly but surely as she widened the gap between her palms, the hole began to expand. "Here we are!" she said as she completed the spellcasting.

"Walk through the portal," said the princess.

My body, controlled by the collar around my neck, began involuntarily to walk through the black hole.

Once inside, I looked back to see that the princess and Lola had followed me through the portal. "Is this place—"

"Yes, this is the vault," said the princess.

This explains why Grandpa and I could never find it—it isn't a room hidden somewhere in the kingdom, or in the tavern itself, but one made of magic hidden in a place where time and space stand still.

I stood in disbelief. Up till now I'd truly thought that I was the most powerful visible magic user in the kingdom, but it seemed that not only had the princess shown me up, but Lola had as well. I hadn't known time and space magic even existed.

Inside the room were rows of bookshelves, with a small wooden table at the center. Lola motioned us towards it. On top of the table was an old, almost charred-looking map of Geatree. The Zaria kingdom sat at the north east corner of the world, while the Goblin and Elf kingdoms both respectively shared a border on the west side of Geatree, with the goblins taking the north western side.

The map was covered in glowing orbs, ranging in colors from red to violet. On the outskirts of Zaria, just near the Lake of Wonders, was a green magical orb. "Hey, what is this orb?" I asked.

"That happens to be your first quest." Lola explained how the orbs marked the location of the kingdom's top secret missions, and how they were sorted by color. The green were the easiest missions, yellow were slightly harder, purple were harder than those, and red were the hardest.

"You mean to tell me that the kingdom's secret bounties and missions have ranking classes as well?" *What doesn't have a ranking in this kingdom?*

Lola placed her finger on top of the glowing green orb and released her magic into it. Once she'd done so, another black portal began to open beside the princess and me.

"Your first mission is to kill a dragon and extract its blood so that the kingdom can determine its origin."

The princess nodded. "Understood."

"Wait! Kill *what*?" I shouted, but before I could finish my sentence, the princess had shoved me face first into the portal, and then followed behind.

As I exited the other side, I found myself falling from the sky. The wind was cold, and oxygen was limited. By instinct, my mouth began to move on its own. "Tempest … tempest … tempest, tempest, tempest, tempest!"

Just before I smashed into the grassy plains, massive amounts of wind swarmed around my body and gently set me down. "That was a close one, but where's the princess?"

Thump!

The princess landed on top of my neck, ultimately causing me to smash into the ground.

The way she landed caused my head to end up under her dress, and my face was between her thighs. I could feel all the blood in my body rush to my face as I shouted. "Mhhhh!"

She stood up, giving me a good look at the sacred cloth between her legs. Her underwear was white, and it had little pieces of lace that ran across it.

How cute.

"What are you staring at?" the princess shouted, stomping her foot on my face.

"Bwah! Jeez, you don't have to be so cruel. Aren't we here to hunt a dragon? How do you plan on doing that in a dress anyway?"

"You're right. I guess I'll have to change into my adventurer uniform."

The princess once again put her hands on the amethyst crystal at the end of her necklace and chanted a spell. As per usual when she cast magic, a bright white light blinded me, and when I was finally able to see again, she looked completely different.

Her dress had vanished, and she had strapped on some boots. Her upper hips, as well as the lower half of her thighs, were exposed to the sun. Her white skin glistened in the reflection of the nearby lake and into my eyes.

Covering her chest was a light brown crop top that almost looked seductive. There were three small gaps in the crop top between her breasts and under them where her skin poked through.

It wasn't until now that I truly took in how beautiful she was, and that her breasts were very nice and pert.

The cropped shirt only covered the top half of her chest, leaving her stomach exposed. Towards the top of the shirt, there was a thin strap that wrapped around the back of her neck, and a thicker strap that wrapped around her back. The bottom of the garment stopped just above her belly button. Her jean-like shorts were narrow around her thighs and hips, leaving most of them exposed. The cropped shirt was so tight against her skin that I could see the outline of her chest clear as day. Around her waist there was a purple leather strap that reminded me of the gargoyle's skin. On the strap was a sheath that contained a shiny blue dagger.

I couldn't believe my eyes. My heart began to flutter, and I could feel my face heating up.

"What's the matter? Something wrong?" she asked.

I sprung up, trying to look confident. "No, no, nothing is wrong, princess!" I said, while putting on my best smile.

"Good. Now let's get going—we have a dragon to hunt."

Chapter 3
A Curse From
Hell

Keiko and Valentina had started their search for the mythical beast near the Lake of Wonders.

We'd been walking for about an hour. The three suns of Geatree were at their highest points, and I couldn't help but sweat. My tongue was dry and my throat was begging for a sip of water. "Hey, princess, I'm gonna unwind and hop in the lake real quick."

"We can't stop now! We have to find the dragon and obtain the blood samples."

Uninspired by her lousy response, I ignored her statement and made my way down toward the edge of the lake. The water was a sparkling blue, reminding me of the princess's eyes. I took a long hard look deep into the lake, but unfortunately I was unable to see the bottom. I couldn't help but scratch my head in curiosity. *Hmmm ... strange.*

I undid the strap on my sash and removed one of the vials, then I dipped my hand into the water. After a few seconds of filling up the vial, my hand started to rapidly heat up. The high temperature of the water became so immeasurably painful that I jumped backwards whilst shouting in agony.

The princess bolted towards the lake with a clear look of concern on her face. "Keiko! Are you okay? What happened?" she shouted.

"Yeah, I'm fine. The water just became oddly hot."

"You're not fine! Look at your hand, it's bright red."

I looked up at the princess's concerned face. I couldn't help but laugh.

As I'd been raised an orphan, my life hadn't exactly been the easiest. When I was younger, I used to get tortured by the local townsfolk. Even though Grandpa Mist and I had lived deep in the woods that bordered the Zaria kingdom, every now and then I would sneak off to the nearby village.

I spent days hunting wild boar and mega wolves in order to skin them. I did my best to hide my wolf-like ears by creating cloaks and hats out of the skinned animals. As a child, I so desperately wanted to be accepted by others that I even went as far as slime hunting.

Magic users are capable of detecting other magic users by picking up on their scent, but I discovered that when I doused myself in clear slime goo I was able to mask my scent and draw less attention to myself.

Although I had many successful trips to the village, every so often the townsfolk would notice my ears or comment on the way I smelt. It was those actions that had led to me being tortured to the brink of death.

Upon discovery, I would be dragged by the townsfolk into a nearby blacksmith and my body would be burned with hot iron tools. They would pluck the nails from my fingertips, and even went as far as to try and burn my ears off with magic.

The curse of the demihumans went deeper than just being considered bad luck to one's own family. At birth, we demihumans had a curse placed on us. No matter the level of magic, or the physical abilities of any being in this world, not a single soul was capable of removing a demihuman's ears. It was the single factor that separated the humans from the demihumans.

They tried cutting them with sharp blades, burning them off, and one townsman even tried to rip my ears from my head with his bare hands. On good days I would just be beaten and left to die outside the village, but as a child who so hopelessly wanted to be accepted, I found it in my heart to forgive them every single time.

The only good thing to come out of that village was the ability to use healing magic. If it weren't for them, I might never have learned.

Looking back, I could see that I had been foolish to ever believe that a demihuman and a human could accept one another, which is why I found it hard to believe that the princess had a shred of emotion behind those kisses of hers.

"Oh it's nothing, princess, dont worry about it."

I smiled reassuringly in her direction, but for some odd reason she didn't accept it. She kneeled down beside me, grabbed my arm and placed my hand between her palms. "Princess, what are you—"

She shushed me into silence. "Just sit still."

I lightly shook my head while rolling my eyes. *Whatever.*

The princess shut her eyes and took a deep breath. As she exhaled, a magical circle began to mark itself out on the burn. A similar circle also appeared on the center of her chest, right above her heart.

Once again, an aura of magic could be seen radiating off her skin, highlighting every curve of her gorgeous body with its green elegance.

She started to sing. Her voice was delicate; it reminded me of a dandelion. When blown by the breeze, a dandelion carelessly and gracefully releases its seeds into the atmosphere, creating a beautiful sight. Her voice, just like the dandelion, seemed so lovely and graceful.

While the princess was singing her song, the pain and the burn on my hand slowly started to fade away, as if they were never there to begin with. After what seemed like an eternity of peace had gone by, the burn on my hand was completely gone and the princess had finished her song.

I looked directly into the princess's eyes while leaning my head in close by only a few inches. As I did so, my face began to heat up, but not from the heat of the sun, no—this was something else. *This girl is amazing.* I thought. Her level of healing magic outranks mine by a landslide.

She reached over to the vial of water I'd spilled on the lakeshore and picked it up. "Here, I think you dropped this."

The vial sat comfortably in the center of her soft white hand. Her glossy clear nails highlighted the vessel's smooth edges.

"Thank you," I said.

I took the vial from her hand and took a sip of the water remaining in it. I picked up the cork and popped it back in. The princess stared at me. Shortly after I'd put away the vial, she began to question me about my necklace.

"Hey, Keiko."

"What is it, princess?"

"What's that chain tucked under your collar?"

I looked down towards the dog tags that hung from my necklace and gathered them in my right hand. A small tear began to form in my right eye. Once I realized the tear was welling up, I wiped it away and changed the subject.

"Speaking of the collar, I find it to be quite humiliating. I may have the ears of a wolf, but I am no dog to be collared!"

I stood my ground while pointing at the princess. "This collar has been nothing but itchy and annoying. There has to be some way to fix it!"

The princess stood up, rested her hands on the edge of the collar and told me to place my hand on her bracelet as well. I was annoyed, but because of the collar's control I ended up doing as she said.

She then whispered the word "luss" into her palm, and in the blink of an eye, both the collar and bracelet had disappeared from our bodies.

"Wait, does this mean?"

"No—you're still my maid. I just used a cloaking spell on your collar and my bracelet. It removes all signs of the objects, and their physical touch as well."

Damn. I was hoping she had a change of heart about the whole maid situation.

"Well thanks, I guess."

I lifted my head towards the sun and brushed back my messy hair. I began to think about the lake, as it was not an unfamiliar sight for me. Grandpa had brought me to the Lake of Wonders once before when I was a child, and I clearly recalled it being lukewarm, not piping hot.

The fact that I couldn't see the bottom also got me thinking back. I remember being able to see the bottom clear as day. *Has the sand in the lake become more dense, to the point where it would have darkened in color? Or has algae maybe started to grow at the bottom of the lake? No, that doesn't make sense, there isn't a single plant on the lake bed, so there's no way algae could have grown.*

I was lost in a trance. While I sat in thought, the princess had taken it upon herself to glance into the lake as well.

She bent over on one knee with her nose just above the water, and smelled it. *What in the world is she doing?*

"Hey Keiko, come here."

I shrugged my shoulders. *Eh, what do I have to lose?* I made my way towards the princess. "What's up?"

"Do you smell that?"

"Smell what?" I asked.

"Do you smell magic? It's coming from the lake."

Now that she mentioned it, I did smell some magic on my hand before, after dipping it in the water, but I was too preoccupied with the pain to even consider the cause of it.

"Yeah actually, I do. What is that?" All the hair on my body, including my ears, suddenly rose. A chill shot down my spine. The princess stood up and focused on the water. Her mood had changed from curious to serious.

"Keiko back up, I'm gonna blast the lake."

"Uh … what?"

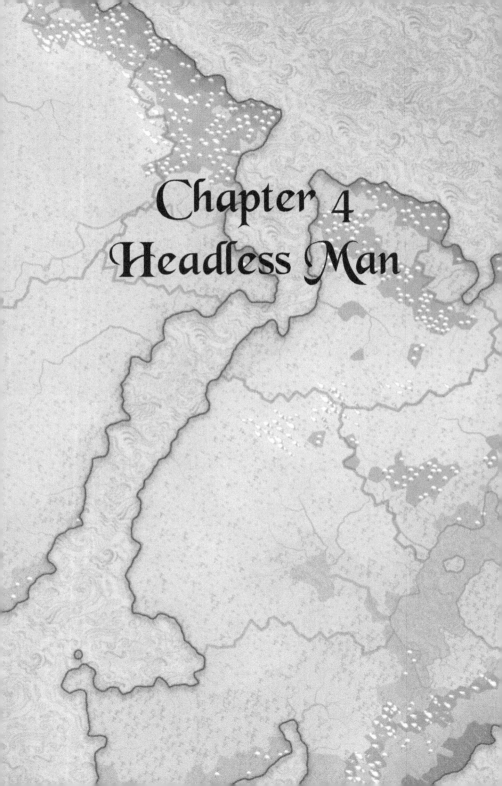

Chapter 4
Headless Man

When I look at the princess, I can never really tell what's going through her mind. Some of the things she's done so far have been quite impulsive, not to mention suspicious, and they have led us to be placed in some bizarre situations. Such as when I was hiding in a corner while the walls of a tavern were collapsing around me.

In the princess's defense, what she has done up until now has been quite useful, but I never fully understand what is going through her head, or why she does what she does. Even so, what she had just said had to be some of the most ridiculous crap I had ever heard in my entire life.

"What the hell do you mean, *blast the lake?* Do you want to cause a small tsunami? You'll end up killing any living thing within five miles of this place with your magic!"

The princess ignored me. Instead, she focused her attention further into the lake.

Here we go ignoring me again. Whatever.

"Keiko, let me see that handkerchief you have in your back pocket."

"What? No. What do you need that for?" As the princess spoke her command, the slave collar around my neck activated, causing me to unwillingly hand over my handkerchief.

The princess reached toward my hand, placing her soft feminine fingers on the handkerchief. She then put the red cloth on the ground next to the lake. After she'd laid it out, she removed her dagger from its sheath and asked me to kneel beside her.

I rolled my eyes, but eventually I kneeled down, since I had no choice. Whether I wanted to or not, I had to obey her commands.

I set my knees into the firm grass on the edge of the lake. It gave off a strong tingly feeling, as if poking through the tears in my jeans. As the grass kissed my skin, I began to get a stronger sense of the magic that the princess had mentioned earlier. *Something definitely doesn't feel right.*

The princess asked me to hand her a vial. I removed a onel from my satchel and handed it to her as instructed.

"Take a deep breath, this is going to hurt," said the princess.

What's going to hurt?

Without hesitation, the princess took her dagger and shoved it into my left ear.

As the dagger entered the center of my ear, a sudden burst of pain and anger made its way from my chest to my lips. "Ahhhhh! What the hell was that for?" I shouted.

In the heat of the moment, all the blood in my body seemed to rise to the surface, causing my skin to shift from pale to blush pink.

I tried to get up in a rage, but as I did the princess shouted, "Freeze!"

What happened next was easy to predict. Just as she commanded, my body froze.

I was now sitting on the ground, unable to move, with a dagger impaled through my ear.

The princess picked up the vial and positioned it next to my ear, just underneath the dagger. Then with her right hand she ripped the dagger out of my ear, and as she did so, thick crimson blood began to ooze out and drip into the vial.

As my ears were immortal, it was only a matter of seconds before they were healed, but the pain remained until my body recognized that my ears had fully recovered.

I had always questioned the princess's actions, but now I was starting to get agitated.

"You may now unfreeze," said the princess.

My body was slowly released from the control of the collar, allowing me to move ever so slightly. Eventually, I was able to completely move my legs. I jolted up off the ground in anger. "What the hell was that for?" I shouted.

"Just watch."

The princess then took the vial of blood and poured it onto the red handkerchief. She then placed her palm into the center of the blood and whispered the words,

"Ostende mihi viam."

As she chanted her spell, three large strands of pure white magic began to seep from the blood-covered handkerchief.

One of the strands seeped into the princess's body, and one into my own. The third strand seemed to flow down towards the bottom of the lake, while ten smaller strands seeped into the nearby forest. "Just as I thought—the source of this magic smell is coming from the lake."

"So you're telling me that spell is capable of tracing magic?"

The princess nodded and began to explain the context of the spell.

When a piece of fabric is doused with the blood of a demi-human's ears, it creates a magical friction. When that friction is combined with the proper chant, it allows the caster to see all the strands of magic in the surrounding area. *If what she's saying is true, that means we aren't alone.*

I recovered my handkerchief and dipped it in the lake. Once the blood was completely washed off, I placed the cloth back in my pocket.

I looked over at the princess. She had her arms held out towards the center of the lake. Shortly afterwards she began to chant a spell: "I call upon the heavenly angels of..."

I guess she really is gonna blast this thing. I gotta find somewhere to hide before I get erased from existence!

All of a sudden, I felt a sensation in the tips of my ears. I looked north towards the forest, where the ten strands of magic had led. I couldn't help but feel uneasy.

It wasn't long until a feeling of curiosity entered my mind. Since the princess was preoccupied with casting her spell, I took it upon myself to find the cause of my uneasiness.

I slowly stepped away from the princess while doing my best to keep quiet so she didn't notice my disappearance. After a silent walk, I eventually made my way to the edge of the forest, where the trees came down to the open fields.

As I got closer to the tree line, my nose began to twitch. Magic was pouring into my nostrils at a rapid rate. I entered the forest and prepared for the worst.

On my stash, there rested four vials; two of them had already been used. One for drinking water, and the other for the blood spell. The other two vials contained a bright purple liquid.

The liquid was thick, and although it looked delicious, any non-magic users would have serious health complications if they tried to consume it. This poisonous liquid was none other than dragon's blood.

I removed one of the vials from my sash and popped the cork off the top. The smell simmered out from the glass cylinder, making its way directly into my nostrils.

Looking at dragon's blood, you'd think it would have a beautiful scent, but the smell was strong enough to burn your nose hairs off. My nostrils once again began to twitch from the smell, and as they did so, the corner of my mouth creased up in disgust.

"Well … bottoms up."

I took the vial and placed it on the edge of my lips. I then leaned my head backwards, allowing the blood to pour into my mouth and down my throat.

The taste was horrid, and the sight of the blood leaving the glass vessel and entering my throat was a tad nauseating, but it had to be done.

Dragon's blood, unlike that of other mythical beasts, contained keystones. Keystones are small magical elements that allow any living creature who swallows them to vanish into smoke and become one with the atmosphere.

Dragon's blood was a hard item to come across, especially

since there hadn't been a dragon sighting in years.

Grandpa Mist and I happened to obtain these vials in one of our robberies. Our goal was to save them in case one of us were ever thrown in jail—that way, each of us could sneak in and rescue the other, but unfortunately, I had never been given the chance to save Grandpa.

My stomach began to clench. I got the strong feeling that my gut was trying to tell me something dangerous was up ahead.

Just as I finished drinking the blood, a large cloud of black smoke began to emerge from my mouth, and it consumed my body from the inside out.

As the smoke devoured me, I could feel the weight of my body start to disappear. It was only a few moments until I was completely infused into the atmosphere.

Up until now, I had never used the dragon's blood for invisibility. The feeling was something I had never experienced.

My body felt light, almost like a feather. My vision had changed as well; I was able to see all forms of magic without the use of a spell. The world was a mixture of black and gray, and all traces of magic were now visibly white.

I started to venture deep into the forest. I could still hear the princess chanting her spell from afar.

"...bring about strength and..."

As I made my way deeper into the forest, the ten magical strands grew thicker. They eventually became one giant ball of iridescent magic. The ball was quite large, reaching over seven feet in height and width. *This is it, the cause of the magic strands.*

As the dragon's blood had changed my vision, I found it difficult to see what was at the center of the magic sphere without getting any closer.

The effects of the dragon's blood didn't last very long. I slowly approached the glowing orb while doing my best to stay hidden.

As I got closer to the sphere, I was able to make out the shape of the creature standing in the center. It had a human-like form. It stood on two legs, had a torso and large muscular arms.

The creature's entire body looked to be made from some sort of raven-black metal. It wasn't until further inspection that I noticed that its head was missing.

It was at that moment that the effects of the dragon's blood started to wear off. My body began to feel heavier, and my vision slowly returned back to its normal state, leaving me fully visible beside the headless creature.

With my vision now fully restored, I was able to properly make it out. The magic trail was caused by none other than a headless knight, and the metal I had seen happened to be its jagged armor.

Like many magical creatures, the headless knights had been created by the elves long ago. The fact that one still existed and had been roaming around undetected for all this time caused a feeling of shock to run through me.

While still staring at the headless knight, I came to the realization that I was fully visible. "Oh shit…"

I took off running towards the edge of the forest, and as I did so the knight followed. For such a large creature, wearing such heavy gear, it was easily able to keep pace with me.

The sound of its heavy footsteps thumping behind me echoed throughout the forest. Birds of all sizes flew out of their nests in fear of the noise.

My legs felt heavy and my vision started to go dark. *Could this be a side effect of the dragon's blood? I can't pass out now! I can't die here, not like this.*

With every last bit of will remaining in my body, I forced my eyes to remain open. *If only I could kill him with magic!*

The headless knights, unlike the other races, were wielders of dark magic.

Dark magic, unlike normal magic, has no visible form or spells that can be cast with it. It simply is an invisible force that prevents all normal magic from having an effect on the creature or object that it possesses.

When a person possessing normal magic comes into contact with a dark magic user, the dark magic user will go on an uncontrollable rampage until the normal magic user has been fully consumed by the dark magic.

The only way to destroy dark magic is to kill the host, by obliterating its soul without the use of magic.

After about a minute of running, I could finally see the edge of the forest. I was on the brink, my vision growing dark, and my legs were quickly weakening. I was desperate; the dragon's blood had drained me of all my magical energy. I was using every last bit of strength left in my body to keep running.

The knight was catching up to me, I had no other option but to keep going. My feet smacked the ground harder than they ever had before.

I could see it—the edge of the forest.

As I leaped out of the woods, I gathered the last of my strength and called out to the princess.

"Valentina … help … me…"

Before I knew it, I was out cold. Unable to move, and unable to fight.

Chapter 5
A Damaged Soul

Where am I? I can't see anything. It was cold, and the air was thin. Tingling sensations ran over the surface of my body. *What is this place?*

I couldn't see a single thing. Confusion spread through my mind. If it weren't for my leather jacket, I might have frozen to death by now.

I looked around the blank space and saw nothing but utter darkness. Scared and alone, I had no choice but to explore the blackness in the hope of finding out what was going on.

I began to walk forwards, and as I did so little splashes began to flick up beneath my boots. It was hard to see, but I could tell that I was stepping in water.

No matter the direction I turned, everywhere I went there was a small amount of water on the floor.

"Brrrrr…" I could feel my body begin to shiver. I was trembling from head to toe.

"Hello … is anybody there?" As I exhaled, the frigid air condensed around my breath, causing a thin white vapor to seep out from between my lips.

Thump… Thump… Thump

What was that? It sounded like the headless knight's footsteps.

Cling!

That sound…

It reminded me of two hard metal objects clashing together.

I was confused, but as there wasn't much that I could do, I stood there quietly listening to the clashing sound.

Eventually I heard a familiar voice.

"Get away from him—him—him—" The voice echoed through the darkness. Its familiarity brought chills to my spine.

"Who said that?" I shouted. I got no response.

Once again, the voice rang out. "Ahhhhh!"

"Who's there?" I asked. Just as before, I heard nothing in return.

"Leave Keiko alone!" said the voice. *Is that… the princess talking?*

My mind was in a state of confusion. The sound of metal objects clashing continued for what seemed like an eternity.

I continued to walk for some time. It wasn't until I felt a stroke of air brush against the back of my neck that I stopped. All the hairs on my body stood up at the touch of the warm, sudden breeze.

Woosh...

What was that?

I glanced behind me, only to see a small, flickering blue light. Without hesitation, I ran towards it.

My boots sloshed in the water, and the loud repetitive sounds echoed in the surrounding void.

As I got closer to the small light, I happened to notice that its features looked human; in fact, the closer I got to it, the more I noticed its resemblance to a small child.

It had black eyes, and tiny arms that paired perfectly with its stubby legs. Its body was round, almost like a small lump of dough. Its head had a similar shape. It reminded me of a small fire, like the ones you see sitting on the top of candles. It was a tiny flame, with a tiny face to match.

What is this flame-child doing here… in this land of darkness and water?

I got closer to the flame, but then it disappeared. *Where did it go?*

Woosh…

"Huh?"

Once again, I felt a warm breeze brush against the back of my neck. I glanced behind me, only to pause.

As I turned around, a trail of little blue flames started to appear, along what I assumed was a pathway through the water. With nothing to lose, I followed the flames without hesitation.

My boots once again were splashing in the water. If it weren't for their leather consistency, my socks would have been soaked. I followed the flames for quite a distance. While doing so, I was able to once again hear the princess's voice.

"I command you to die!"

I couldn't help but wonder to myself: *is she fighting the knight?*

It crossed my mind that while I was carelessly walking around this void, the princess was alone.

She may have possessed powerful magic, but that wouldn't help her against a dark magic user. I had yet to see her fight without the use of magic.

If there was one thing I was confident about, It was my ability to wield any kind of weapon. *She could be hurt.*

I thought about escaping the void and helping the princess, but as I did so a darker thought crossed my mind—*if the princess's magic is consumed by the headless knight, then ... wouldn't that release me from the collar's control?*

I blocked that thought and furiously shook my head. The fact that I could think of letting the princess die for the sake of my freedom filled me with disgust. *I can't believe that I would think such horrid things.*

I started to run as fast as I could in the direction of the flames. As I passed the flames they disappeared behind me, while at the same time even more started to appear ahead of me.

Is this an endless trail of misery? I thought. *It can't be. She needs my help.*

The sound of metal clashing together got louder and louder

until I finally reached the end of the path. In front of me was a large sphere of glowing light—half of it was yellow, and the other half was black. Afraid to approach it, I froze.

My arms were trembling with fear. I wasn't one to typically get scared, but I was in an unfamiliar place. I might be alone, but that was nothing new.

The small flame-child once again appeared, but this time it was on my shoulder. I glanced towards it. The little flame floated towards the giant glowing light. It raised its short stubby arm and pointed in the direction of the orb.

"You want me to touch it?" I asked.

The flame nodded.

I gulped down the remaining saliva in the back of my throat. "Okay." I said.

I walked up to the multi-colored orb. I placed my right hand on the line where the two colors met, and almost instantly my head began to pound and my vision went blurry. *What's happening to me?*

A strong, cold burst of air forced its way into my ears.

Whoooooosh!

The wind was roaring and the pain was unbearable—I couldn't help but scream. I opened my eyes and looked directly at the center of the orb. Both the yellow and the black halves were sending a flow of energy into my hand.

My eyes began to bulge out of their sockets, and my hands started to tense up into fists. I shouted in pain. "Ahhhhhhh!"

After a few minutes, my vision began to get really bright, and I couldn't see anything except a beaming yellow light.

I was struck by a stark feeling of concern. *Am I... blind?*

Eventually the light dimmed, and when it did I saw...

"Grandpa...? Is that you?" *What is this?*

I was floating, and my body was transparent. I looked to the left, then back to the right. I appeared to be in my childhood home, and Grandpa was there too.

I tried to speak, but my voice went unheard. I was unable to move much. There seemed to be some kind of invisible barrier holding me in place.

"Grandpa! Grandpa!" I shouted.

I began to bang on the walls of the barrier while calling out for my grandfather.

"Grandpa please... help me!"

I dropped to the floor of the barrier. Tears started to well in my eyes.

Why am I here? Did I deserve this? Is this the consequence of drinking dragon blood? Am I... dead?

The tears began to roll down my cheeks and onto my hands. I wiped them from my puffy eyes while desperately trying to calm myself down.

I felt a familiar gust of wind brush the back of my neck once more. *Woosh...*

I suddenly glanced up.

In front of my face was one of the little blue flames that had brought me to this place. It pointed down towards Grandpa.

"I know, I already saw him," I said, still wiping the remaining tears from my face.

A soft voice, almost a whisper, filled the room. "Look closer," the voice said.

I once again glanced down towards my childhood home. *Huh… is that… me?*

To my surprise, I saw myself as a mere child. I think I must have been eight at the time. I was talking to Grandpa.

"Now listen," the soft voice said.

As instructed, I placed my ear on the wall of the barrier to hear what was being said.

***

"Keiko, it's okay to be who you are. You don't have to force yourself to be someone you're not, just to get the approval of others," Grandpa was saying to the younger me.

***

I remember this. This was the time he caught me dousing myself in slime goo, so that I wouldn't be noticed in the village.

***

"Keiko, you are a strong young man. Don't let your past or the actions of your mother change you into someone you are not."

"But Grandpa, I'm cursed," said my younger self.

"No, Keiko—you are blessed. For some reason, the gods of Geatree chose you to be a demihuman. The gods don't mess up, they never have. So be yourself, put down the slime goo and show them the Keiko that I know: the kind, innovative and adventurous Keiko."

***

I remember that conversation.

At the time, I think I was too young to truly understand the meaning behind Grandpa's words. After Grandpa's death, up until I met the princess, I had been stealing valuable items from people with the sole purpose of causing despair. I wanted them to fall into a state of anger and hopelessness, to experience payback for all the pain they caused me. I wasn't stealing to survive anymore, I was stealing for revenge.

I dropped to my knees. I couldn't believe how far I had let

myself fall into the pit of despair after Grandpa's death. *When did I lose myself in all this anger? How long ago was it?*

I now fully understood what Grandpa was trying to tell me back then. I had changed for the worse, not to appeal to people, but because of my resentment towards them. I began to plead with my grandpa, even though he couldn't hear me.

"Grandpa, I'm sorry. Please forgive me. I'll change, I swear I'll make up for the wrongs I've caused! I'll fix all my mistakes!"

My tear-filled eyes quivered at the sight of my reflection through the barrier. My soul was destroyed; I had hit rock bottom.

The room faded back to the black void it once was.

Just as I thought about giving up on returning to the princess, the little blue flame placed his hand on my cheek, causing my tears to dry into thin vapor. I looked into his dark, empty eyes. "Thank you, little flame."

The flame released his grip on my face and pointed in the direction of the orb.

What's happening?

As I stood there in the cold shallow water, facing the glowing sphere, cracks of orange light could be seen breaking its way through the black half of the orb.

Underneath the blackness was an orange light. Eventually, the black half was put under so much pressure that it exploded. I covered my eyes with my arm to protect them from the blast.

Boom!

My feet slid backwards only a couple of feet. After the explosion, I removed my arm from my eyes, revealing a new, multi-colored sphere.

Half of it was yellow, and the other half orange. The black emptiness of the void started to slowly shift colors. The surrounding area was no longer dark, but now a beautiful vibrant white. I could see now clear as day. I walked towards the newly-colored orb. I couldn't help but feel a strange connection to it. "That must mean that this is…"

I looked over towards the flame once more. It nodded.

"—my soul."

The once-dark half of the orb happened to be my soul. *Was I consumed by darkness for that long?*

The yellow half of the orb looked so innocent and pure. *If the black half of the soul was mine, then this half must be ... the princess's.*

She mentioned that the spell she cast bound us to each other by connecting our souls as one. I swore then that I would do everything in my power to make sure that her soul stayed pure, and never fell to the darkness.

I moved my hand outwards towards the combined souls. As I did, I could hear the princess's screams.

"Somebody, help!"

Her screams echoed through the newly-bright void. Dark purple cracks began to appear on her half of our soul. "Dark magic! The headless knight must be consuming her magic. I have to go."

I looked over towards the tiny blue flame, only to drop to my knees and beg for a way out.

"Please little one, show me the way out of here."

The flame-child once again raised its tiny arm in the air, and as it did so, a glowing door appeared in the center of our souls. Without hesitation, I opened the door and stepped through it, and as I did, I heard a voice.

"Farewell, grandson. Make me proud."

Wait— "Grandpa?"

Strong winds grabbed hold of my legs. The doorway was sucking me back into the world. I grabbed the edge of the door and pulled myself up with everything I had left in me. I could feel the weight of a thousand men bearing down on my arms, but I didn't let go. I pulled myself up to the door jamb, just enough to where my eyes could see past the trim and into the void.

The little blue flame-child sat floating in the open, waving its stubby little hand in my direction. I looked towards it. A large gust of light swamped it, and as it faded I saw a figure, and that figure was Grandpa. There was nothing but a smile on his face.

He was here all along.

A single tear fell from the corner of my eye.

"I'll make you proud, Grandpa. I will."

The weight of the wind became too much. My arms gave out and I was sucked through the door. The force was enormous, pushing me through with ease.

I'll right my wrongs, Grandpa, and I'll start with saving the princess.

My vision went blank, and eventually I blacked out.

When I woke, my body felt stronger than ever. I was in the exact spot that I had passed out the first time. Not a single scratch or bruise was on my body.

I was still a little dizzy. I stood up and brushed myself off. I looked over towards the princess. She was lying on her back and the headless knight was on top of her. Dark magic was coming out of his empty neck armor, where his head should be, and seeping into the princess's mouth.

The sight of the knight tarnishing the purity of the princess's soul caused an eruption of anger in my chest.

I could feel every last part of me tingling with magic. My body began to glow orange, and as it did, a bright light appeared in the center of my chest.

I reached into the light, only to feel a metal handle at its focal point. I grabbed onto the handle and pulled outwards.

Out of the core of my chest emerged a bright orange katana. The handle was black, and it had red tassels hanging from it. Pure, visible magic was pouring out from both the blade and the arm I held it with. I couldn't help but chuckle with my trademark cheeky smile.

"Don't worry, princess, I'm gonna send this knight back to the pit of hell from whence he came."

Chapter 6
Legendary Battle

After confronting his past, Keiko was able to abolish his sins and truly connect to the princess, causing a katana to be forged from the bond of their two souls.

I rushed towards the headless knight, screaming in anger at the sight of it corrupting the princess's pure soul with its dark magic.

"Ahhhhhh!"

As I rushed towards them, I could feel my body being enhanced with every step I took closer to the princess. *Is this the true power of our master and maid bond?*

The veins in my arm began to pump full of magic.

I could feel the intensity of the sword rushing through my body. My heart began to race, and my eyes bulged. It felt like the magic of a thousand men was rushing deep into my soul, but it wasn't that, it was the princess's magic merging with my own.

I had the headless knight in my sights. My legs were running faster than they ever had before, the soft thin grass trampled beneath my feet. I was furious and ready to let all hell break loose. *I'm running fast, but not fast enough.*

"Tempest," I whispered.

Woosh!

At my command, my spell caused a strong gust of wind to swirl around my body, allowing me to increase the speed at which I was running. Flowers of all kinds had their petals stripped away as I darted past.

I could see the princess clearly. Her face was slowly turning black, and her veins were beginning to clog in her neck. Her eyes were rolling back in her head.

This is not good, I have to get there in time!

"Ahhhhhhhh!"

At the sound of my scream, the princess managed to collect whatever strength she had left and look in my direction. Her eyes widened slightly at my appearance.

It was hard to tell if she were surprised or scared.

Her lips quivered, and water began to well up in her eyes. As I got closer, I heard her struggle to whisper the words, "Kill him."

The invisible collar around my neck glowed blue as she gave me her command, before fading back to nothing.

"Oh ... it's game time!"

Cling!

The knight's heavy black armor echoed as the katana came down hard.

Cling, cling, cling ... cling, cling!

The katana clashing against the heavy armor caused the grass in the surrounding area to sway backwards. Hit after hit after hit, the knight absorbed them all.

I need to get stronger—this sword is good but there is no way I can beat him in this state.

I swung my sword at the knight's right shoulder, but it was deflected by its dark magic armor. Before I could pull the sword back for another attack, it grabbed the blade with its right hand. Slowly, the knight began to pour its dark magic into the katana. The once-orange sword began to fall to the knight's darkness. Sweat seeped out of my pores at the sight of the katana suffering defeat. *No... no... no! I can't do it! I can't beat him. His dark magic is too powerful.*

Doubts began to run through my head, until I looked over at

the princess. She was barely awake, and it was obvious that the dark magic was still consuming her soul. Even so, she was continuing to fight it with everything she had.

She looked over at me, and we locked eyes. She smiled, just before suffering a burst of uncontrollable agony. Foam formed at the edges of her mouth, and her eyes rolled right back. I needed to do it, I needed to beat the knight. I let out a huge angry roar. "Ahhhhhhh!"

Think Keiko, think!

I released my left hand's tight grip on the sword, and lifted it upwards until it was directly in line with the passing clouds. Then I shouted out a spell more powerful than any that I had ever cast before.

"Tonitura!"

Within a fraction of a second, blue lightning bolts shot down from the clouds, striking me directly in the top of my head. My eyes turned from orange to blue as the lightning struck.

Small sparks of electricity shot out of my skin and into the surrounding area, setting fire to anything it touched. I gripped the sword—almost fully hidden by the flames—with both my hands and shouted once again, except this time it wasnt out of anger, it was a shout of power. "Ahhhhh!"

Boom!

Waves of dark magic shot across the landscape, as the lightning magic flushed it out of the sword. Every blade of grass, every plant and tree within a one mile radius, was instantly turned to ash.

My tempest spell was still active. That, combined with the lightning and the katana, allowed me to gain total control over the headless knight's movements.

Blood was rushing through my body; so was the magic of the katana and both spells. I could feel my skin getting thicker and my heart beating even faster.

With the power of my tempest spell, I was able to fly in towards the knight and grab it by the collar of its breastplate. I gripped the armor as hard as I could while dragging the knight through the dirt. I then lifted it into the sky. As I did, electricity was making its way out of my body and into its armor.

Even though the regular magic was unable to destroy the dark magic, it was still able to damage the knight itself. The knight's armor began to glow red as its temperature rapidly increased.

Although it had no head, I could tell that the knight was in pain. It grabbed my arm with both of its hot metal gloves.

The lightning spell was starting to show signs of being a double-edged sword. It allowed me to quickly blast surges of electricity into the knight's body, but at the cost of burning myself where I touched the knight.

The spot on my arm that the knight was holding on to, as well as the hand that was holding on to its metal collar, began to smell like burnt skin. Pain was rushing through my arm.

I could feel my heartbeat through the melted flesh on my arm, but that didn't stop me. I continued to fly higher and higher, until I couldn't physically fly anymore. Once at the height of my limits, I reached my arm behind my head and arched my back. Then, with all the strength in my body, I leaned forwards as fast as I could while swinging my arm down and released my hold on the knight, causing it to be hurled down towards the ground.

I could once again feel the magic of the katana bursting through my veins. It was time to release it.

"Tempest."

I flung myself downwards in a spiral, while holding the bright orange sword out in front of me. My ears pierced the wind sharply as it raced through the hair on my head, and my jacket was ruffled, as was the rest of my clothing. "This is for the princess!" I shouted.

Just as I did so, the katana entered the gaping hole where the knight's head should have been, and pierced through the hard shield of dark magic that surrounded its core.

As the katana came in contact with the core, the knight violently slammed into the ground, causing the earth beneath it to shake. The force of gravity, paired with my own strength, created an intense explosion as the katana burst through the center of the knight's thick purple shield.

Boom!

The blast was strong enough to send me flying backwards. I dropped the katana in the explosion, and as a result, it faded back into the center of my chest, while the two spells I had cast immediately vanished. I slammed into the ground head first, causing the grassy earth in the surrounding area to break free from the rest of the soil.

My body slid across the ground until I finally crashed into the princess. She wrapped her soft, tender arms around my body as we tumbled towards the lake. We came to a sudden stop just before falling into the scorching water, which for some reason was literally boiling.

The princess and I were wrapped in each other's arms, allowing me to feel her heartbeat. Her heart was racing, just like mine.

"Is the knight dead?" I asked. "Please tell me it's dead."

The collar around my neck and the bracelet around her arm both appeared from thin air and glowed blue. They disappeared shortly after.

"Yes, it's dead," the princess said. "You completed your task. Good job."

The veins on the princess's neck began to fade back into her beautiful white skin as her face returned to its original color. Her breathing shifted from heavy to calm.

Out of energy and completely unable to move, I remained on the ground with the princess still wrapped in my arms. The backs of her legs brushed against my inner thighs. She was so close. I was able to smell her hair without effort—it gave off a sweet scent, reminding me of green apples.

Her head was resting on my arm, and her back was pressed up against my chest. My other arm was wrapped around her body, falling just beneath her round, plump chest. At a time like this, I would normally be blushing, but I was too tired to process in my mind the position we were in. I let out a deep sigh as my breathing slowly began to return to its normal pace.

"Hey, Keiko."

"What is it, princess?"

"Thanks for saving me. You really are the best maid ever."

The sound of her words brought a smile to my face. I started to chuckle, but stopped as it caused a sharp pain to shoot through my lungs. "I am beat."

The princess laughed. "Me too. Keiko…"

"What is it?"

"What was that sword you pulled out of your chest during the fight? It was strange, but the sight of you pulling that sword out of your body made the inside of my chest feel all tingly. Almost as if we increased our bond on a spiritual level."

Even though she was facing away from me, I could tell she was blushing. I was able to see the edges of the princess's ears turn red as she asked me the question.

So, she felt it too, I thought to myself.

I rested there in silence for a bit, then spoke. "Oh? So you expect me to answer all your questions while you ignore mine. It's a secret," I said in a teasing tone.

The princess rotated her body until our faces met. Her eyes locked onto mine, just as they always did right before she kissed me.

My ears perked up, and my face began to feel hot and sweaty. Before I knew it, the princess had punched me in the center of my chest where the sword had come out. Sore from the battle, I felt the pain of her punch even more intensely than usual.

"Idiot," she said, pouting.

We both laughed.

"I deserved that," I said.

The princess snuggled up closer to my immobile body. "How come you saved me?" she asked. "You could easily have let me die and gained your freedom from my spell."

I let out a thick gust of air from my lungs. "Everybody has their reasons for fighting, and even though you won't tell me yours, watching you try so hard to reach your goals is a good enough reason for me to do everything in my power to protect you. That and the fact that you commanded me to, so it's not like I had a choice!"

The princess giggled. "Alright, it's time we get back to our main goal: finding the dragon and slaughtering it so we can collect a blood sample."

The princess stood up and cast a spell. I was too weak to cast any healing spells of my own, and the princess was still recovering from the dark magic that had attacked her soul. The best thing she could conjure up was a carrier spell.

My body once again felt lighter than a feather. The spell she'd cast caused me to float next to her as she moved.

The three suns were still shining brightly and the weather was beautiful, but the screams we could hear in the distance were anything but.

"Princess, did you hear that?"

"Yeah. It sounded like it was coming from nearby."

The princess looked at me. It was clear from the expression on her face that she desperately wanted to run in the direction of the screams. "Let's go," she said.

"But what about finding the dragon?" I asked.

"That can wait till later. There are people in trouble!"

The princess took off running, and once again I found myself involuntarily following behind.

Chapter 7
Trail of Screams

Huff ... huff ... huff....

I could hear the princess breathing heavily as she darted towards the screams. She flattened the sharp grass with every step she took. I was currently floating alongside the princess, unable to move. I don't know how I'd activated it, but the use of that katana had taken a toll on my body.

Because I was bound to the princess, everywhere she went I was forced to go as well, due to the control of her master and maid spell. Honestly, I didn't mind it; I was basically getting a free ride and some time to rest, and the wind felt great in my hair. It helped me cool down my body temperature.

I was still sweaty from the fight with the headless knight, so it was very relaxing. That was until the princess changed course, from running in the open fields to going through the forest that bordered the plains.

The princess ran through the forest, her mind fully focused on finding where the screams were coming from. She had tunnel vision, her mind was blank and she had gone into a hyper-driven state.

I looked over at the princess, and as I did I couldn't help but feel a sense of warmth. *Wow. She really is serious about finding the origin of these screams.*

I couldn't name a single person who would run into the unknown at the sound of screaming to help somebody they didn't know. *If only the people of the kingdom had her kind heart. Then maybe ... just maybe ... I would have been accepted.*

I directed my attention back to the direction in which the princess was running. To my surprise, I was greeted by a tree branch.

"Waah..."

Thump!

"Ouch..."

Bang!

"Gaah..."

Tink!

"Bwaah..."

Thud!

"Princess! For the sake of..."

103

Boink!

"... the heavens please..."

Crack!

"... put me down!"

She couldn't hear me. She was focused on one thing and one thing only, finding the source of the screams. As we got deeper into the forest, the screaming got louder and louder. My face was constantly being pummeled by the branches that were sticking out of the trees.

Leaves and twigs of all sizes entered my mouth, nose, and hair, and some of them even poked near my eyes. Between all the various leaves and plants battering at my eyes, I was able to catch sight of the princess's movements. There was something odd about her. Every now and then, she would lift her head higher than usual. She reminded me of an animal hunting its prey.

We got closer to the screams, and as we did so I could smell a familiar scent.

Sniff... sniff

Wait… is that…?

The princess brushed through an overgrown bush. The twigs and leaves once again smashed up against my face.

As we exited the bush, we were greeted by a young girl. Her cheeks were puffy and covered in tears, making it hard to see those little spheres she called her eyes. *She must have been crying for a while now.*

The girl was kneeling down on a small patch of gravel. Her body was covered in dirt from head to toe. The only thing covering her bare skin was a potato sack that had small holes cut out for her arms and legs.

She had no shoes or pants. Her arms were covered in small cuts and her hands were bruised. The dirt in her hair made it impossible to tell the original color. *Is she alone?*

Without hesitation, the princess picked up the girl and embraced her. She looked so young, possibly eight or nine years old. "Calm down, cutie, it's okay," said the princess.

The girl continued to sob her heart out on the princess's shoulder. "Hey, you're not alone anymore. You don't need to cry."

The little girl increased her grip on the princess's shirt. It was clear to me that this girl was an orphan, maybe even a slave who had escaped being sold. As I looked down at the little girl, my heart skipped a beat or two. I couldn't help but feel a sense of connection at that moment; there had been a time in my life when I'd been scared and alone too. If it hadn't been for the warmth of an old man, I may have never made it into my teenage years.

The little girl began to speak with such a soft, shaken voice. "I'm not crying because I'm alone."

The princess looked confused. "Then why are you crying, cutie?"

The little girl released her grip on the princess's shirt and lifted her arm upwards. She was shaking, and her palms looked sweaty and bruised. I followed her arm movement closely with my eyes, all the way to the tip of her finger. She was pointing towards an awfully large shrub. "I'm crying… because he's hunting me."

The princess slowly turned her head towards the shrub that the little girl was pointing at. My gaze followed hers. *That smell… I know it's familiar, but what is it?*

The ground beneath us began to vibrate, and leaves fell from the trees. The vibrations in the ground grew stronger. The shrub rustled and shook. All three pairs of our eyes were locked onto the large bush that the little girl had been pointing at. A few seconds went by, and the area once again grew quiet. "Who's hunting you?" the princess whispered.

The little girl lifted her tiny head, placing her lips closer to the princess's ear, and whispered, "A minotaur."

As she whispered her faint words, an oversized half-human bull burst through the shrubbery. My eyes widened at the sight of the minotaur. "You have got to be kidding me," I said.

His glossy blue eyes were angled downwards, and you could hear the ring in his nose as it moved against the hot breath he was so furiously exhaling. The minotaur bent over slightly, only to inhale a large amount of air, causing his chest to expand to nearly double the size it had once been. He lifted his shoulders, along with his head, high in the air. Once his head was at its highest peak, he let out a roar.

"Grrraaauuuuuuuu!"

The force of his roar caused the princess to be lifted off the ground and flown backwards. Her body soared through the air.

Small bits of bark flew everywhere as she smashed into a nearby tree. "Holy shit!"

The carrier spell was undone. As a result, I dropped to the ground, landing in the pile of gravel. My face was now buried in the stones and I was still unable to move.

The minotaur stomped its way over towards the princess and the little girl. The princess hadn't wasted any time. After smashing into the tree, she instantly stood up and took off towards the outskirts of the forest, leaving me alone and defenseless. The minotaur ran past my body, his foot smashing down next to my face. Fear ran down my spine at the sight of the black furry foot. Veins began to burst out of the minotaur's large muscular arms as he ran off after the two girls. Once again, I was able to smell that familiar smell. *Why can't I remember what it is?*

The smell was so potent that it was driving me insane. *I should be focusing on more important things, like getting out of this slump and killing that minotaur, but this smell is driving me crazy!*

I remained face down in the gravel for what felt like an eternity. In the distance, I could hear the princess casting countless spells. Screams from the little girl began to pierce the air.

Frustrated at my inability to move, I began to mumble to myself through the gravel. "I'm an M-A class adventurer and I can't even move my body after using one powerful spell! Ahhh, this is so frustrating!"

Little chunks of hard gravel entered my mouth as I lay there mumbling. The taste of the gravel was dull and disgusting.

I spent the next few minutes fighting with myself internally, trying to figure out a way to restore my magical energy. Without it, I wouldn't be of any use to the princess or the little girl. *Think... think... think...*

Then a small bug ran across my fingers, causing them to twitch. "Wait ... I can move my fingers."

The magical energy in my body had restored itself enough to the point where I could move only my fingers. "That's it!"

Eruptido is a spell that is cast by crossing your index finger with your middle finger and submerging the two in water. The spell is a high energy explosive that is typically used for exploding your enemies from the inside out. You fill them with magical energy until their bodies can't handle it, which ultimately leads to a fiery eruption. "If I use this spell on myself, then maybe I can increase my magical energy. I don't know, though, I risk killing myself in the process if I overdo it."

I sat there debating the pros and cons of casting the spell on myself. It wasn't until I heard the little girl in the distance pleading for her life that I decided I was going to cast the spell.

I saw myself in that girl, and I wanted to save her. After all, I'd promised Grandpa I would do everything I possibly could to right my mistakes. "I have no choice! I'm gonna do it."

The only issue was that there was no water around for me to submerge my fingers into. Once again, my thoughts turned into an internal battle. *Think... think... think...*

I crossed my fingers as required by the spell. "Maybe... just maybe this will work."

I began to furiously slosh my tongue around in my mouth, gathering all the saliva onto the edge of my lips.

Here goes nothing.

Ptui!

A large ball of spit left the comfort of my mouth and headed for my fingers. "Eruptido!" I shouted.

My face began to grow warm as the spell took effect. The energy seeped through my body, allowing me to move more of my fingers. I began to rapidly spit on all my fingers and cast the spell over and over again.

Ptui!

"Eruptido!"

Ptui!

"Eruptido!"

Ptui!

"Eruptido!"

Magical energy was now coursing through my body at an unstable rate. Dark smoke began to seep out of my ears. I was almost able to move fully—everything except my legs were back to full functionality. My skin was pale and I felt sick to the point where I could vomit at any moment. *If I go any further I could end up killing myself.*

It was then that I heard the little girl scream for help in the distance. "Helppppppp!"

WIthout hesitation, I shouted louder than I ever had before: "Eruptido!"

Boom!

A massive shockwave caused all the surrounding shrubbery to explode in a fiery eruption. My head was pounding, and my body felt warm.

My vision was hazy from the energy, but as I glanced down towards my arms I noticed that they were clothed in an orange aura. I took a closer look and saw that my whole body was glow-ing.

Unstable eruption magic was bouncing throughout my body. I started to feel my blood boil. My body was hot and I was on the brink of an explosion. One wrong move and I could end up dead. I had to release some of this magic immediately, and I knew just who to release it on.

Chapter 8
The Strenght of a Princess

Princess Valentina's point of view -

My chest felt tight, and my lungs were on the verge of giving out. My arms shook with the discomfort of carrying the little girl. The wind blew my hair in all directions, making it hard to see where I was running to. The sound of the ground cracking beneath extreme amounts of pressure echoed through the forest as the minotaur followed closely behind me. I was exhausted, and still recovering from the headless knight's attack on my magic.

I could hear the minotaur behind me, slowly closing the gap between us. I planted my foot on the ground and pivoted as fast as I could. I grabbed my right arm with my left hand and aimed it at the minotaur. "Ignite!" I shouted.

A small arrow of combat magic sliced through the air and penetrated the minotaur's chest.

Combat magic is a unique form of advanced visible magic. It allows the user to create various weapons from the surrounding area's mana. 'Ignite' is a spell that causes the water vapor in the atmosphere to condense into the shape of an arrow. The pressure of impact upon the arrow hitting its target causes the condensed water vapor to burst on an atomic level, ultimately creating a small explosion.

The speed of the arrow hurling at the minotaur caused a loud whistling noise in my ears.

Boom!

I looked past the smoke, while doing my best to stay on the alert. It was quiet, almost too quiet. I wasn't about to fall for that again. I leaped up just at the right time—the minotaur had hurled a large stone slab at us through the dark smoke.

The little girl began to scream uncontrollably. "He's going to kill us! Help, please. Somebody help!" Tears were flooding down her cheeks once more.

I felt my muscles tense. I clenched my teeth and my face stiffened. *I'm not gonna let this girl die.*

The spell I had cast was nowhere close to being as powerful as the ones I usually did, but I was still exhausted. Eventually I made it to the edge of the forest and back onto the plains. With the trees out of my way, I was now free to let loose without having to be worried about smashing into any of them.

I put the little girl down on her feet and whispered in her ear.

"Wait here, I'll be right back."

She looked up at me with a gloomy expression on her face. "Okay, princess. Be safe."

I placed my hand on the little girl's dirt-covered hair. Underneath all of that mess was a soft little head. I smiled and nodded. "I'll do my best."

I turned around to face the minotaur, but as I did so, a thought entered my head: *How does she know that I'm a princess? The necklace, maybe?*

The minotaur had rushed up behind me as I was putting the little girl down. I wasn't focused; I was too busy questioning how the little girl knew who I was.

The muscles in my stomach tensed up as the minotaur took his large fist and smashed it into my abdomen.

"Blawww!" The pain was so unbearable that blood shot out of my mouth. The impact of the minotaur's punch sent me soaring. The cold wind brushed through my hair, leaving it a mess once more. I was now about sixty feet up in the air. I looked down, only to see the minotaur closing in on the little girl. My eyes bulged as anger filled my soul. "Don't you touch her!" I yelled.

I rotated my body until my head was pointed at the ground and my feet were facing the suns. "Golden scythe!"

'Golden scythe' is a form of light magic. Light magic uses the light projected by one of the three suns and converts it into physical form. By using this spell, I was able to cover all ten of my fingers in light magic. Each finger was equipped with a slightly large claw that resembled the shape of a scythe, hence the name of the spell.

Light magic, unlike other forms of magic, is much weaker during the night. At night, light magic converts the moon's light into a physical form. Spell names also change during the night—'golden scythe' becomes 'darkened scythe.'

I could feel rage bubbling up in my chest. As I was incapable of casting any high class spells at the moment, I figured 'golden scythe' would be my best option, because it relied on the strength of the suns and not on my own.

"Tempest." I kicked the air behind me and blasted myself towards the ground at an immeasurable speed. The sound of the wind whistling in my ears brought a smile to my face. I could see the minotaur getting closer to the little girl. She screamed, and as she did I landed on the minotaur, digging the golden scythe claws into the back of his neck.

I could hear the sound of flesh ripping off the minotaur as I dragged the claws from his neck down his back. He screamed in agony, and I loved it. I began to go into a full-on rampage, swinging my arms as fast I could while slashing at the minotaur

The beast started off helpless, backing up and only blocking, but as time went on I could sense that he was starting to learn my attack patterns. He gave off a look of confidence in his glossy blue eyes right before grabbing my arm and stopping my attack. Blood was oozing down his back and over his arms, leaving his black fur stained crimson. His grip was tight around my forearm, leaving me unable to escape his clutches.

I began to feel dizzy, not of my own doing but because of the minotaur, who'd started swiftly spinning in a circle. He picked up speed. Eventually we were spinning so fast that I could feel myself falling unconscious. *I will not let this little girl die!*

I struggled to keep myself from passing out. Luckily, just as I was about to fall victim to the swift rotation, the minotaur released his grip, causing me to fly directly into the hard rocky ground. The sharp stones beneath the soil surface skimmed across my face, leaving me covered in cuts and bruises.

I clenched my teeth at the unbearable realization that I was too weak to kill this minotaur. *How is he so strong? None of my spells have had a real effect on him. Is he a dark magic user? No, he can't be. Minotaurs are incapable of wielding dark magic. Plus, he doesn't smell like it.*

I began to doubt my power and the ranking given to me by the Adventurers' Guild. *I'm a triple-S rank! Why can't I kill this thing?*

I glanced up at the sound of the little girl pleading for her life. The minotaur was hanging over her, dripping his blood onto her small helpless body. I felt weak and useless.

I sat there and watched as the minotaur grabbed the girl by the front of the potato sack and lifted her up towards his face. Hot steam blew out of his nose and into her eyes. Her little body trembled in fear as the large beast began to choke her.

I can't let her die. "Please, don't die!" I said while struggling to get back to my feet. "That sword. How did Keiko use that sword?"

I managed to get back up. It wasn't until this moment that I noticed Keiko was missing. *That's right. He wasn't able to move, and I just left him there. He could be dead for all I know.*

Golden scythe was still equipped on my fingers. With the suns at a high point in the sky, I had a good chance of beating this thing. It wasn't the spell that was holding me back, it was my own strength and stamina, but I had a goal, and I wasn't going to lose.

With all the strength left in my body, I ran towards the minotaur. I grabbed my dagger out of my sash and shouted a spell. "Infuseis motealoneis!"

The golden scythe claws began to leave my fingers and merge with my dagger. It grew to three times the size it had originally been. It was no longer blue, but now a glowing yellow. I charged towards the minotaur. Sweat ran down my face and my legs.

The minotaur swung his large muscular arm in my direction, landing a hit on the side of my body.

"Blahhhh!" I was flung backwards, but that didn't matter.

I got back up and charged him again. I landed a slash on his upper thigh, only to be hit again. I landed on the ground, wheezing with the pain. *I will not die here!* I stood up once more, and as I did, I caught sight of something that gave me hope.

Keiko had emerged from the forest. His body was glowing. I smiled, and a small tear fell from my right eye as he walked towards the minotaur. I whispered a command. "Keiko, save her...

please."

The bracelet around my arm and the collar around his neck both appeared from thin air, only to glow blue then fade back to nothing. I saw it, and I know he did too.

Keiko's point of view -

Oh? She made it a command, I see. "Don't you worry, princess. I'm gonna kill this son of a bitch!"

Chapter 9
Body, Mind and Soul

Every last fiber of my being was bulging with unstable eruption magic. Little droplets of sweat evaporated the second they left my pores. My eyes were dry to the point where blinking was impossible, and my temperature was steadily increasing.

With every step that I took closer to the minotaur, I could feel the interior of my body slowly start to burn at a greater rate. The orange aura around my body was so bright that I could barely see past it. If any sweat managed to escape evaporation, it was being swept away by the mildly warm breeze.

My legs were shaking with each step I took, and only continued to do so as I held onto the overwhelming amount of explosion magic. The smell of my skin slowly burning off my body reeked unpleasantly. I could feel the flesh on my face melting away with every second that went by.

The three suns shining brightly into my eyes didn't help, either. It was hot and I was ready to pass out.

Looking back on my life, I would say without a doubt that I hadn't been the type to jump the gate on helping someone in need, or even bother helping at all. I was beaten, bruised, and burned all my life just for being different, but when I looked at the princess, I couldn't help but feel encouraged. The way her eyes shimmered just now, and the sense of trust I got when I was around her, it lit a fire in my chest that I can't explain.

My eyes were locked on to the minotaur. Sweat, blood, and tears were slowly seeping out of my body. I was hurting badly. I had to release this magic soon, but the only issue was that the minotaur was holding the little girl by the throat.

His shiny silver ring was fogging up as he blew hot steam out of his nose and onto the young girl's face. The big furry beast had multiple open wounds running down his back; the fact that a creature of his ranking was able to withstand such wounds without flinching was remarkable.

Minotaurs, along with slimes, mega wolves, trolls and wyverns, are all creatures typically assigned to lower ranking adventurers. This was due to the fact that magic was not needed to defeat any of these creatures. Adventures ranked "C" and up were eligible to accept bounties that called for hunting minotaurs. The fact that the one we were currently fighting carried no weapons and had zero protective armor left me baffled.

As I came closer to the minotaur, a familiar scent teased my nose once again.

The little girl had both her tiny hands wrapped around the hand of the ugly beast. Her neck was swelling from the pressure of his grip. Although it was hard to see, I was able to get a clear view of the drool coming out of the little girl's mouth. *Alright, enough waiting. It's time.*

I dug both my feet into the soil beneath the little grass that was left from the previous explosion.

The wind in my hair was the only thing keeping my head cool. I licked my two fingers and expanded my arms out to the side as far as they could stretch. I felt the flesh on my arms slowly melting away. As oozing flesh fell from my arms and onto the ground, I locked my eyes onto the minotaur.

My heart was pounding. It sounded like a caged gorilla bashing its way to freedom. The princess was yelling in my direction, but I couldn't quite hear her. I was too focused on the minotaur. I counted down from three.

Three ... I shut my eyes and inhaled.

Two ... I slammed my hands together and pointed them forwards.

One ... I chanted my spell.

"Eruptido!"

All the unstable energy in my body came forth to the tips of my fingers and surged outwards. A large, brightly-colored orange beam flew swiftly in the direction of the minotaur and the girl.

Wisp!

In the blink of an eye, all the energy and magic that was bouncing uncontrollably around in my body was entering the minotaur through his oversized nose.

The force of the spell hit my body hard. My feet were forcefully sunk deeper into the soil as I slid backwards. I was doing everything in my power not to fall. If I fell back before the minotaur exploded, then this would all have been for nothing. I couldn't help but scream with all the energy flowing out of me.

"Ahhhhhh!"

I could see it, clear as day. The minotaur's body was rapidly expanding. His black fur was burning away from the overwhelming temperature of the blast. His huge muscles expanded even more as mana filled his body.

"Yes… yes… yes!" I screamed.

This feels great! I feel amazing! A smile appeared on my face, and I couldn't help but laugh. In fact, before I knew it I was laughing uncontrollably.

It was hard to hear the princess, but she was yelling in my direction. I didn't care—I had never felt this kind of power before. My heart was racing and my muscles were loving every minute of it. I felt my eyes widening. The smell of my burning flesh no longer lingered in my nose. I was going mad, and I loved every last bit of it. "Blast him more! Blast him… blast him... blast him, blast him, blast him, blast him, blast him!" Manic laughter once again burst from my lips.

My mind was blank, and all my senses besides my sight were completely overcome. I was unable to even feel my fingers. At this point, I didn't know if I still had any. "More power!"

Before I knew it, my body had been tackled to the ground. "Blahhh!" Blood uncontrolably oozed out from my mouth. The princess had her arms wrapped around my chest and the little girl was kneeling by my side.

How did the little girl get over here so quickly? I wondered.

I felt a massive pain in my stomach. I tried to place my hand on it when the unimaginable happened: my hand went right through it. I no longer had a stomach, but instead there was a large blood-filled hole where my stomach should have been.

I began coughing up blood again. I met the princess's gaze. Her eyes were filled with tears, and her body was trembling, but why? I glanced over at the little girl. *There it is, that smell.* If it was what I thought it was, then…

I lifted myself up.

"Stay down!" yelled the princess. "You're badly hurt."

I struggled to speak. Blood was filling my mouth and throat with every passing second. "Where's… the… minotaur?" I asked.

"You killed the minotaur. He exploded from a mana overdose ten minutes ago! You have been firing off that spell ever since then. I've been trying to get you to stop but you weren't listening!" More tears dripped from the princess's eyes.

Am I ... dying? I coughed up even more blood.

I could feel myself on the brink of death. My vision was fading to black and my body felt really heavy.

"Keiko, please! Please keep your eyes open! Please!"

Due to the master and maid spells command, my eyes were forcefully held from shutting, but that didn't mean my vision was stopped from going black. I could barely see what was going on. All I saw were various green illuminating circles appearing around my body. *Is she trying to save me?* I thought. Nobody had ever tried to save me before. Rather than save me, people would leave me to die and rot. It had always been that way, ever since I was born.

My eyes were hazy and I was about ready to give up. My only regret was that I wouldn't be able to fix more of my mistakes. *I'm sorry, Grandpa. I truly am.*

Just as I was saying goodbye to this word, I felt a soft sensation on my crusted lips. It was familiar, it was—the princess. Her tears fell from her cheeks and onto my face. At that moment I felt a warmth radiating out from the center of my chest.

131

Visible magic was powerful, but I had never seen a spell like this one. My body felt light and tingly. The flesh on my arms and face began to mold itself back into its original shape. The gaping hole at the center of my stomach slowly proceeded to close itself. My vision, along with all my other senses, was once again functional. I opened my eyes, and when I did, I was greeted by the princess. Her lips were locked on mine, and she was glowing. The sight was truly beautiful.

Is this healing magic?

I looked down at my body, and I was surprised to see that it had been completely healed. Valentina removed her lips from mine and lifted herself off my chest. "But how?" I asked.

"I thought I lost you, dummy," she said, wiping the tears off her face. "Don't you get it by now? We're connected by our souls. There is no stronger force than that."

I heard a soft voice off to my left. "Are you alright mister?"

I did my best to raise myself. Although I was healed, my body was still in pain. "I will be, after I do this."

"Do what?" the little girl asked.

"Ignite." A small arrow appeared from the water vapor in the air and flung itself into the little girl's body.

The princess's eyes widened in confusion and fear. "Keiko, what are you doing?" she shouted.

I was now fully healed, and the little girl... was dead.

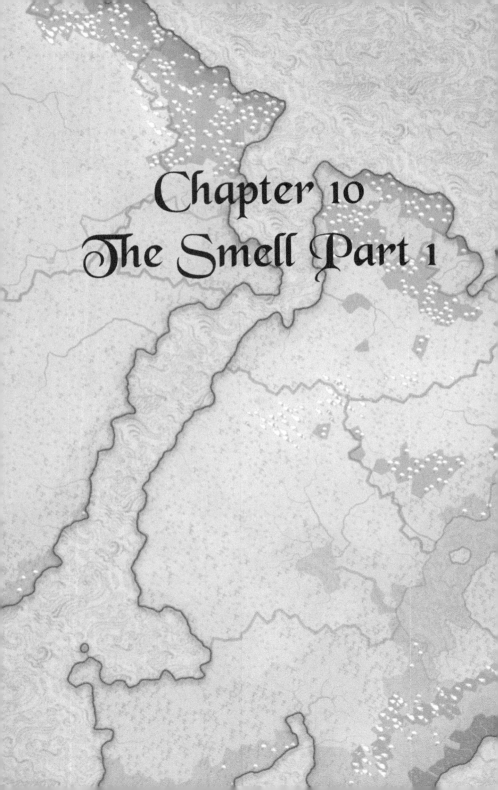

Chapter 10
The Smell Part 1

Keiko had just shot the little girl with a combat spell, leaving Princess Valentina in a state of utter confusion.

Five years earlier -

"Keiko… Keiko!"

"Huh? Yes Grandpa!"

"Keiko! What are you doing digging around in that bag of trash? You're covered in filth."

I giggled. The look on the old man's face was goofy. Grandpa's silver eyes shimmered with warmth.

I ran up to him in excitement. "Look, Grandpa, look! Look at what I found."

In my hands rested a blazing green jewel. Although its edges were sharp and jagged, the overall texture of the jewel was smooth and fine to the touch.

"What do you have there Keiko?" Grandpa asked, smiling.

"It's a green jewel, grandpa! I found it in the trash bag!"

Grandpa's lips suddenly trembled. "Keiko—where did you get that trash bag?" he asked.

"I grabbed the bag from behind the blacksmith in the neighboring village. They didn't notice me because I was covered in slime goo," I laughed. I couldn't help smiling; this was the first time I had ever found anything valuable in the trash.

I looked up at the old man. His face was pale and his eyelids were quivering. *Is something wrong?* I wondered.

"Keiko, take that jewel and return it to the village at once! I can't afford to have the village guards knocking on my door when they realize that a precious jewel has gone missing. If you are going to steal, tell me first so I can scout the area for witnesses.

"But Grandpa, I—"

"Enough! We are not going to talk about this. Go and return it now!"

I lowered my ears in sadness. My heart had dropped and a feeling of coldness had overcome my body. All I wanted to do was to make Grandpa happy. I'd spent days searching through the garbage for the sake of finding him a gift. After all, he was the only one who accepted me for who I was… and all I'd done was make him mad.

It was a long tiring hike, but I made my way back to the village. I was out of slime goo and had nothing to cover the stench of my magic. *I have to make this quick so that nobody notices me.*

While approaching the village, I did my best to remain unnoticed. The only spell I could use was 'tempest,' and even so, I was still learning how to control it.

The village had a select few of their residents patrolling the borders every now and then to ensure that no intruders could enter. I squatted behind a bush, making sure that no one could see me.

Dang! How am I going to put this back now?

I glanced to my right in the direction of the blacksmith shop. Vivid memories of torture and pain rose from the depths of my thoughts. I felt nauseous, to the point where I could have thrown up. Every time I saw that blacksmith, I was reminded of the brutal reality of being a demihuman.

Focus, Keiko! If it means making Grandpa happy, then you

have to return this jewel.

I did my best to conjure up a tempest spell with the intention of distracting the guards patrolling the area.

I whispered, "Tempest." Nothing happened. *Come on, I can do it!* "Tempest," I said again. Still nothing.

I sighed. "I can't give up just yet!" I locked my gaze on the center of my palm. I closed my right hand and whispered the word 'tempest' into it. Then, with all the air remaining in my lungs, I blew into my palm.

My eyes lit up at the sight of the spell's magical aura leaving my hand. I looked over towards the guards and watched the spell brush along the back of one guard's neck.

"Huh? Who's there?" he said.

"What are you talking about?" the other guard asked.

They began to ramble on in confusion. *Now is my chance!* While the guards were busy arguing, I took full advantage of my opportunity to sneak past them and enter the village.

As soon as I made it past the guards, I darted towards the

blacksmith's. My legs were moving at a rapid pace, and my ears were tucked back as far as possible in the hope of preventing anyone from noticing them.

Luckily, I managed to make it to the blacksmith's shop without being noticed. I ran behind the old stone building to where I had found the trash bag. Just as I went to place the jewel on the ground, I heard an unfamiliar voice coming from the old creaky window above.

"Somebody help me! Please, I beg of you!"

"Shut up!"

My ears twitched with curiosity. On the outside of the building there were three overly-large wooden crates. I put the jewel down beside a nearby bush and pushed the crates together. Eventually, I managed to create a makeshift staircase.

I put my hands on the edge of the smallest crate while placing my foot in the openings of the other three crates. I felt a tingly sensation between my toes as I placed them on the mossy edges of the nearest crate.

I managed to climb my way to the top of the stack. It was just tall enough to enable me to peek through the window. What I saw next was nothing short of a surprise.

"Please... I... didn't take... your jewel." It was a young girl. A demihuman nonetheless. She was covered in blood and pinned to the wall by her fox-like ears. She was screaming in pain and terror as the blacksmith burned her chest with a hot iron rod.

"Oh yeah! Who else stole my jewel then, huh? A *human*?"

"I don't know... please, just let me go." The girl said, with tears flooding down her face.

The blacksmith hit the girl with a slap so fast it seemed to slice the wind. The girl again screamed from the immense pain.

My heart skipped for a brief moment. This poor girl was suffering because I had taken the jewel. Of course he would blame the first demihuman he found. She was young, probably my age.

"Tempest." I used the spell to quickly float the jewel up from the bush and into my hands.

"Fine. If you won't tell me who stole the jewel, then I'm just gonna have to kill you!"

My eyes, and the girl's, both widened. *There's no way. The people of this village only torture demihumans, they never kill them!*

The thought of this girl dying because of a mistake I had made left me in a state of panic. *I have to help her. I can't let her die. Not here, not like this.*

I hesitated. The sight of the girl's thick crimson blood running down her face and body left me in fear. I had suffered that same fate plenty of times, and yet, I never got used to the pain.

The blacksmith approached the young fox-girl with a large rusty pole that he had just pulled from the furnace. Hot sparks were falling off the end of the pole. The girl's eyes widened once more. Her mouth opened wide as she begged for her life.

"Please mister, please! I didn't do anything wrong."

Tears were flooding her eyes, and her cheeks were flushed red. She was unable to move her hands. The blacksmith had chained them to the wall. They were high enough to keep her hanging, but low enough to put all the pressure of her weight on her ears.

My heart pounded at the unholy sight. He was going to kill her, and all I could do was watch.

He approached the young girl with the red hot pole. As he walked, the floorboards creaked and crackled. A creepy smile appeared on his round, chunky face. Greasy sweat dripped off his bald head and onto the girl's half naked body. Her clothes were torn, and the little skin that was showing was covered in blood.

My body was frozen. I couldn't move a muscle—I was in total fear. The blacksmith took the pole and brushed it against the girl's ears.

The smell of burning flesh filled the room. The girl screamed, but was silenced by a large, greasy rag that the man had shoved in her mouth.

"Mmmmphhhh!"

"Now, it's time to die, you filthy animal!"

In an instant, the blacksmith had taken the rusty pole and shoved it deep into the stomach of the demihuman girl.

"Mmmmphhhh!"

She tried to scream, but her voice was muffled by the rag. The red steel of the hot pole began to burn her flesh from the inside out. All the hair on my body stood up in shock.

I thought about Grandpa and how he'd taken me in. The warm home he'd provided for me, the clothes he'd managed to steal for me, and the food he was able to provide for me. At that moment, all I wanted to do was share the warmth of Grandpa's smile with that girl.

She glanced in my direction while screaming. We locked eyes. She couldn't speak, but it was clear from her gaze that she was ready to give up and accept her fate, and that's when it struck me hard. *Why am I just sitting here? I have to help her!*

I had been selfish. Worrying about my own life over a girl who was in danger. I clenched both my teeth and my fist alike.

"Get away from her!" I shouted, jumping through the window.

The blacksmith turned in my direction. He recognized me easily. It was no surprise as I had been chained to that wall plenty of times.

"My jewel! So it was you, Keiko!"

"This is no time for conversation! Let her go now!" I demanded.

He just smiled. "Alright, I'll let her go, but first hand me the jewel."

I was conflicted. I had no way of telling if he would let her go if I gave him the jewel. For all I knew he could be lying. Sweat ran down my arm and onto the shiny green surface of the jewel.

He pushed the pole deeper into the stomach of the girl.

"Mmmmphhhh!"

"The longer you keep me waiting, the further in I'm going to push it."

"Alright, alright. I'll give it to you, just stop!"

The greasy man smiled cheekily. The menacing look on his face caused my body to shake in fear. Adrenaline was rushing through my veins. I struggled to do so, but eventually, I threw the jewel on the floor next to the blacksmith.

He walked over to it slowly. The girl was still chained to the wall with the pole inside her. Her eyes began to fade from red to black, and her face was turning pale.

"Hurry up already!" I shouted. The faster he claimed his jewel, the faster she could get down and I could heal her. I was still unable to use healing magic, but I carried around a healing potion. It was the only thing that saved me from dying when I was tortured in this village.

"Be quiet. I'm getting to it," he said.

I could tell that the girl's life force was draining away. *Screw it!*

I bolted past the blacksmith and over to the girl. I ripped the pole from her stomach and undid the chains around her hands. After doing so, I removed the sharp knives from her ears, allowing her to fall into my arms.

"Hey! Who said you could release her like that?"

The blacksmith charged me and the girl. I made my way towards the window, only to leap from it at full speed.

"Tempest!" I shouted.

Please work!

A gust of wind lifted my body. My magic was drained from

the spells I had cast before, leaving this spell to only last a few seconds.

The spell gave out and I dropped to the floor. I landed on my knees, causing them to get dirty. I struggled to stand up while holding the girl.

I removed the cloth from her mouth and wrapped it around her stomach. It was covered in grease, but it was the only way I was going to stop the bleeding.

As night had begun to fall, I started to lose track of where I was headed. I had unintentionally rushed to the center of the village. *Crap! Not good.*

I was now exposing myself to all the townsfolk. One demihuman running around was bad, but now there were two of us. The people of the village started to point and yell.

"Leave our village, you demihuman trash!"

"Yeah. Don't come back here you unholy beings!"

The words of the townsfolk hit deep in my heart. Small tears began to form in my eyes. *Stop crying, you loser! This girl is dying and you're going to let some stupid words get to you? How*

146

pathetic.

I headed towards the village exit. As I did so, I couldn't help but notice that this beautiful young girl had a peculiar smell to her. Her long orange hair wrapped around my arms while blowing in the wind.

I looked down into her hazy red eyes, and that's when I noticed a change.

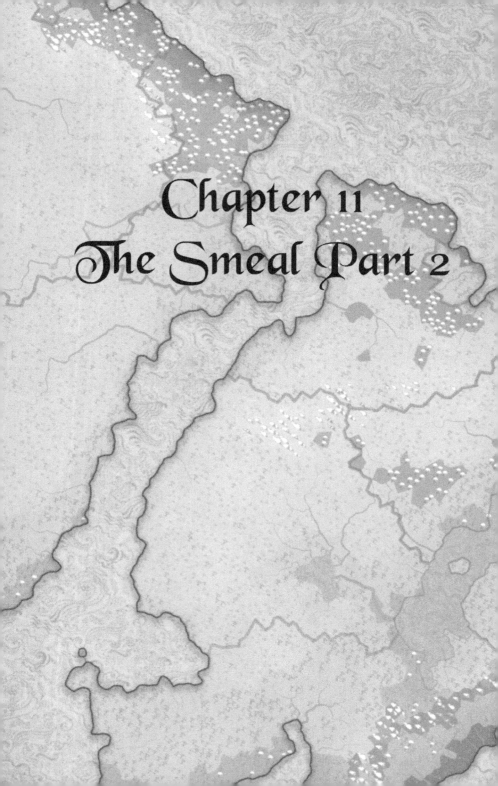

Chapter 11
The Smeal Part 2

Townsfolk from every corner of the village, who rarely left the comfort of their homes were now outside taunting me and this poor girl.

My hands were doused in her blood. She was covered in it from head to toe. The cold night air embraced my lungs with open arms, making it harder to breathe. I looked down towards the bloody girl.

I pondered her unusual smell. It was odd for a demihuman to smell like she did. She didn't smell of visible magic; instead, she smelled different. I was too preoccupied with the townsfolk to look any further into the situation. I had to escape the danger of the village.

It was one thing for me to be tortured and beaten by the towns-folk, but for this poor girl to be tortured because of my wrong doing was unacceptable.

I ran as fast as I possibly could, even using the assistance of my tempest spell to help me gain some speed.

Eventually, I made it to the water fountain on the northeast edge of the town. In order for the healing potion to work the user had to be hydrated, or else it wouldn't take effect.

I quickly set the girl down on the ledge of the fountain, then popped the lid off the vial containing the potion. I took the girl's chin and held her mouth open. She was barely conscious. The skin on her face was almost completely flushed. She was dying, and it was up to me to save her.

I only had the one vial, and the potion couldn't be used without the victim being hydrated first. "I guess I have no choice!"

I shoved my head into the fountain and took a large gulp of water, being careful not to swallow it. It was then that I heard a faint whisper to my left.

"Please, help… me."

"Mhmmm!" I shouted with a mouth full of water.

I grabbed the blood-covered girl by the shoulders and positioned her body closer to mine, her face right in front of me. I hadn't realized it before, but under all that blood was a cute, fragile girl.

This is no time for thoughts like that, Keiko! Well… here goes nothing.

I moved the girl's face closer to mine, and as anybody would have done, I kissed her. Our lips locked without any passion. I was doing my best to remain calm, but nothing could stop my face from flushing.

I felt my body's temperature begin to elevate. I couldn't help it, this was my first kiss. *Her lips are so... soft.*

I held her lips open with my tongue the best I could, allowing an easy path for the water to exit my mouth and enter hers. Luckily, she swallowed it.

Gulp.

"Perfect. Now all that I have to do is give her the potion! Wait, where's the potion?"

I began to panic once again. I checked every pocket and fold in my clothing.

"Where is the potion? I know I put it around here somewhere!" I started to hyperventilate. "Where is the potion?" I yelled.

"Oh... you mean this little old thing?"

I slowly looked up from the center of the fountain. *The pitch of that voice. The smug sound it made when leaving its owner's mouth. Don't tell me…*

I glanced to my right and there he was—the blacksmith. He had a smug look on his big round face. "I think this is what you're looking for," he said.

In his right hand was my vial, containing the healing potion. I felt all my hope quickly fade away.

"Give it to me… please."

"What was that, kid? You're going to have to speak up if you want this potion!"

With my head held down, looking at the floor, I slowly walked towards the greasy old man. "Please… give me the potion."

"I don't think I will. Tell me kid, why should I give it to you?"

I began to stumble over my own words. "She's… dy… dying… please."

He laughed. There was not a shred of decency in this man. No morals, no empathy, and no perception of life. I stopped walking. My body filled with rage. I could feel immense amounts of magical energy swarming around inside of me.

"What did we ever do to you?" I asked, clenching my fist.

He licked the chapped parts of his lips with his thick creepy tongue. His eyes locked on to mine. I could tell just by looking at him that what he was about to say, he meant with every bone in his body. "You were born."

I clenched my fist even tighter than before. The magical energy in my body began to pulsate. I felt it beaming through my veins and muscles. My chest tightened, and I could feel my lungs consuming more oxygen than they normally did. Just as I was about to break, the girl did something unbelievable.

"Skahhhhhh!"

A loud screeching noise burrowed itself into the depths of my eardrums. The look on the blacksmith's face changed. He had a clear look of concern. I quickly turned around, and when I did, I saw an unholy sight.

Her skin had started to bubble, and those bubbles only grew in size. What once was her right arm was now a large glob of dark navy sludge. Her body began to morph from an innocent little girl into a ball of oozing slime.

"What the heck is going on?' I shouted. I looked at the black-smith, but he was just as confused as I was. Everyone in the village started to panic. They grabbed their torches and their pitchforks, and launched them at the giant pile of sludge.

Thoughts entered my mind at an unpleasantly rapid rate—*what is this? Where did the girl go? What's with the sludge?*

The ball of slime began to grow even larger. It swallowed the torches and pitchforks with ease. Bubbles of all sizes started to explode on the surface of the creature. I had never seen anything like it. This wasn't any normal slime; whatever this thing was, it was clear that it was hostile.

"Help... me."

"Wait. Is she still alive?" I asked in shock.

I looked over towards the blacksmith in anger. "What the hell was on the edge of that metal pole?"

He had frozen, only to pass out shortly after. I glanced up to-wards where the plea for help had come from. There was some-thing at the top of the massive slime. *Wait... is that...?*

My eyes widened at the horrendous sight. The little girl's head was infused into the top of the slime. Her eyes were rolled back, and she was screaming in agony. I wanted to throw up. I felt nauseous just looking at her.

This poor girl. What do I do now? A healing potion isn't going to fix that!

"Don't worry! I'll save you." I had no idea what to do.

Think Keiko! Think!

My mind was blank. I couldn't think of how to save her. I didn't even know what type of creature I was dealing with. The smell of her magical essence became so overwhelming that even a person who possessed no magic could smell it.

I fell to my knees at the realization that I had taken everything from this girl. *She was on the brink of death because of me.* "If I had just not taken that stupid jewel! Then this never would have happened."

Pathetic, isn't it, Keiko? You said you were going to help her, and now look at the situation.

The creature began to swallow everything in sight. From bushes and trees, to food carts and even townsfolk.

She grabbed the blacksmith with her slimy tentacle and tossed him into the air.

"Help me!" he shouted. "Keiko, I'm sorry! Just help me please!"

My shoulders shrugged as I laughed at him. "Funny, where have I heard that before?"

Just like that, the blacksmith was swallowed by the giant pile of sludge. The creature left a trail of ooze behind it as it started to rampage. No human was safe.

"Help me… please."

It was her voice again. Those soft fragile lips were begging for a second chance, but there was nothing that I could do. I felt useless and unworthy.

No, Keiko. You can help her, you just have to try!

It was too early to give up. When I looked at the giant pile of goo tearing apart the village, I got flashbacks of her sad teary eyes. She wanted to live, and it was up to me to save her. "Maybe, just maybe, this healing potion will work!"

I positioned my bare feet on the rough gravel road at the edge of the fountain. I picked up the vial that the blacksmith had dropped on the grass before he'd been eaten. I then looked the pile of slime right in the eyes and charged forwards.

"Tempest!"

Woosh!

I took off flying. This was the first time I had done so successfully. I positioned the hand with the vial in front of my body. "I have to do it... for her!"

I flew faster and faster. I continued to cast the tempest spell while it was already activated in a desperate attempt to increase my speed. If I was going to penetrate that thing, then I needed to be going fast. It wasn't enough just to penetrate it, I had to reach its stomach; that way it couldn't instantly digest the potion.

"Tempest... tempest... tempest... tempest... tempest... tempest... tempest... tempest... tempest... tempest!"

I was screaming at the top of my lungs. I was flying so fast, almost to the point of falling unconscious. The wind was swiftly swirling around my body, creating a mini cyclone. The power

I felt running through my body was like nothing I had ever felt before.

I was a mere inch away from penetrating the surface of the slime when the unthinkable happened. It disappeared.

"What? Where did it go?"

Crash!

"Gahhhh!"

My face had just slammed into the stone face of the church. I dropped to the ground.

"Ahhhh! That hurt." *Wait... where's the slime, and where is the girl?*

I heard a growl to my left. "You have got to be kidding me."

The giant slime ball had shrunk down into a new form: it was no longer a ball, but now a slime wyvern. The little girl's head had now morphed into the wyvern's back.

"Please... help me." Her eyes rolled back once again.

"I'm trying my best, but I just don't know what to do!" I had never seen a creature shapeshift like that before. That's when it hit me.

When Grandpa Mist had first taken me in, he would tell me stories about creatures that he had encountered all over the land of Geatree. According to Grandpa, and a couple myths I had read in a book, there existed a creature known as a shapeshifter. Grandpa had never actually come into contact with one of them, but apparently somebody in his old adventurer crew had.

According to Grandpa, his friend had nearly died from this shapeshifter. They had a unique smell and were impossible for non-magic users to point out.

Shapeshifters required a host to live. Without the use of a host, they would wilt and die. The shapeshifter itself was a small parasitic worm that took over the brain of its host. It then injected their body with a neurotoxin that allowed it to control their brain. They pumped their host's body full of stem cells, which allowed it to morph into any given creature that it saw fit. If that were true, then it would explain why the girl was able to turn into such a large slime-like creature.

According to a couple of myths that I had read in a book,

shapeshifters were common in young slaves. As they grow up in uncontrolled environments, they are subject to more diseases and parasites.

Does that mean that this girl was a slave? That would explain her tattered clothing. *Does this mean that the blacksmith bought her for his own personal use?*

The thought of what he was planning to do to her pissed me off. *If that blacksmith wasn't already dead, I would kill that son of a bitch!*

"If I'm correct, and a shapeshifter has taken control of that girl's body, then there's only one thing that I can do. I have to kill her."

Chapter 12
The Smell Part 3

Body morphing parasites, otherwise known as shapeshifters. They mainly targeted slaves or creatures of no magic. A shapeshifter had one purpose in life: to eat. Once a shapeshifter had taken over a host, they went crazy with hunger, and the only way to stop a shapeshifter from eating was to kill it.

Ninety percent of the time, if a shapeshifter had taken over a host, that host was most likely dead. By injecting the host's brain with poisonous toxins, the shapeshifter took control of the nervous system, which led to the death of the host. That was something that I had learned.

The sound of fires burning brought life to the quiet night sky.

Drip... drip... drip.

Dark-navy goo was falling from the shapeshifter's body into the cracks of the stone pathway beneath its feet. Bubbles of various sizes oozed out a mixture of sludge and blood.

The girl had a ten percent chance of still being alive. I couldn't possibly fathom the amount of pain she must have been going through. For all I knew, the parasite could be the one making her beg for help as an attempt to lure people in.

I hated to admit it, but it was a good thing that the townsfolk detested demihumans. If it weren't for that, many more of them might possibly have ended up being tricked into becoming a quick meal.

The parasitic wyvern struggled to fly. The weight from the overwhelming amount of goo surrounding its body must have been weighing it down.

I stared long and hard, doing my best to analyze the situation I was in. The town was on fire, and the heat was blazing. *I could try burning it. No, that won't work, it swallowed those torches whole, flame and all.*

I was a good distance from the water fountain, so drowning the creature was out of the question. I had one last idea. *If I can't burn it, and I can't drown it, then I guess I'm just going to have to slice it.*

Even though Grandpa was incapable of wielding magic, his friend Jax from his old adventuring squad could. Before Jax died, he would visit me and Grandpa. One day, out of the blue, he'd brought me a book as a present.

It was old and worn out. The cover was faded and the leather around the edges was starting to peel off. It was the only re-maining copy of *The Book of Spells*. How he'd gotten his hands on such a treasure baffled me, but I knew not to ask questions around Jax. He was a shady man who dealt with shady people, but he had a good heart.

If it weren't for Jax, I might have never attempted to use magic in the first place. I recalled a spell that went by the name of 'black flame.'

'Black flame,' like the spell 'ignite,' was a form of combat magic. 'Black flame' was just as it sounded: it surrounded the user's body in a mass of black fire. With the proper control, the user of the spell would be able to slice through anything, living or nonliving, no matter the strength of its composition. The only problem with the spell was that the user had to remain calm while using it, otherwise the spell's mana would overwhelm the user and they would burn to death.

It's my only choice! I have to do it.

If there was any chance that the little girl was still alive, then I wanted to do my best to save her.

I stared at the slime wyvern. Townsfolk from every corner of the town were doing their best to destroy the monster. The heat from the nearby fire was warming my body. I was already hot and sweaty from the failed attack I had just attempted.

"Here goes nothing."

I spread my arms to the side, just as the spell instructed. As I did so, I noticed that the shapeshifter had once again caught sight of me. It placed its small wings on the ground and positioned its legs in a stance screaming that it was ready to charge. If there was one thing that a shape shifter needed, it was food, and I was a buffet just waiting to be eaten.

The shapeshifter kicked its rear legs, causing dust to fly everywhere. *Funny, the second it stops attacking the villagers and charges at me, the townsfolk stop caring. I guess that's just how things are, and how they'll always be.*

The creature was closing the distance between us at an incredible rate. I had to hurry up and finish the spell. I felt a shock course through my body. I shut my eyes to block out the sight of the shapeshifter. I had to remain calm.

My heart was beating out of my chest, and the heat from the fire wasn't helping the situation either. I took a deep breath, allowing a thin layer of frost in the air to enter my lungs. As I exhaled, I began to calm down.

I could hear the wet footsteps of the shapeshifter as it ran towards me. I took another breath, this time doing my best to block out the sound of the outside world.

She was the only other demihuman that I had ever seen; I didn't want her to suffer such a cruel fate. I continued to take deep breaths as the shapeshifter charged my still body. It was hard to hear, but the drool from its mouth made a faint splashing noise when it hit the ground as it came.

I wonder what she looks like when she smiles? What kind of food does she like? What's her favorite color?

She's not just a demihuman, she's a living being with hopes and dreams. I focused on my breathing, just to the point where my heart rate went back to normal. At the same time I was channeling my magical energy into both palms.

Be one with the flame... channel your energy... focus...

The image of the blacksmith torturing her, the fact that she had been sold as a slave, the blood that had been running down her body as she begged for my help, and the look in her eyes as they rolled into the back of her head were all things that should have angered me, but instead I remained calm. I used all these things as fuel for my fire.

Five seconds...

The sound of its footsteps echoed in my ears.

Four seconds...

The ugly growl it made sounded nothing short of devilish.

Three seconds...

The heat from my internal anger warmed the center of my palms.

Two seconds...

A rash breeze brushed through my hair.

One second...

The creature was close, very close. I smiled.

Now...

I opened my eyes.

Vssssvvmph!

Dark-colored sludge was flung everywhere. Strong winds sliced through the surrounding buildings and trees, chopping them in two.

"It... worked? It worked!" I started to jump frantically with joy. My adrenaline was high and excitement filled my soul. "That's right! The girl, where is her body?"

I looked to the left, then back to the right. The girl's body was nowhere to be seen. "No... please don't tell me that I—"

Just as I was about to cry, a familiar scent caused my nose to twitch.

Sniff... Sniff...

My eyes widened; it had to be her. I started to run through the crowd of townsfolk standing nearby. They started to yell and throw things at me. To them I was no better than the shapeshifter.

Goo was stuck in my hair and dripping down my face. The force of the spell had caused blood to shoot out from my nose and onto my arms, but I didn't care.

Her scent was getting stronger. I ran and ran and ran some more, until finally … I found her. The girl was facedown in the dirt. Her body was surrounded by townsfolk.

I did my best to push my way through them, but they shoved me down. My body was sore from the spell, and I had little to no mana left. The people of the town were angry. They were searching for someone to blame. Who better than the girl whose body had been used for shapeshifting?

I started to tremble at the sight. They picked up stones and launched them in her direction. As if the stones weren't enough, some villagers took it upon themselves to stab the girl's body with sticks.

Why… why… why… why… why… why…?

"Why?" I shouted. "What did she ever do to you? Stop it!" I was screaming so hard that I could feel the veins in my neck tugging alongside my muscles.

They kicked me and they held me back. They had their hands wrapped around my arms, and their knees pushed up against my back. I was useless, unable to set myself free from their clutches.

One of the townsfolk grabbed my hair and ripped it upwards.

"Ack!"

A painful shock shot across my scalp. Blood began to drip from the top of my head, down to my eyes. I could see the girl's face, but there were no tears in her eyes.

Why isn't she crying?

She tried to whisper, but it went unheard. I focused in on her lips. She said it one more time.

"Thank... you... for... releasing... me..."

My heart stopped—and so did hers. The only difference was that mine only skipped a beat, hers didn't.

My face was numb. The energy in my body gave out and I stopped resisting. They punched me and they kicked me. I never even knew her name. *I will never forgive you!*

That day is the day something changed inside of me. I no longer wanted to fit in, no... I wanted to kill them all. That's how it was until I met the princess.

Present -

"Keiko! What did you just do?" The princess had started to freak out. Her eyes quivered and her body was frozen.

Gurgle!

She quickly glanced at the little girl. Dark navy sludge had begun to seep out of the rips in the potato sack clothing she was wearing. Her arm began to spin in a circular motion, and then it exploded. Goo shot out, onto the princess's face.

Her shoulders lifted and her fingers twitched. "What the heck was that?"

"A shapeshifter—I recognized the smell." I couldn't look the princess in the eyes. The navy goo covering her body reminded me of the little girl. Just like this one, I'd never learned her name.

"A shapeshifter? I thought those were just myths?" The princess got up off the ground.

I looked down at my leather boots and let out a small laugh. *It's funny, the people who needed my help the most ended up dying because of me.*

"I wish that was the case, princess. I wish it was."

She placed her soft hand on my shoulder and leaned in until her chest was touching my back. "Keiko—are you okay? Is something upsetting you?"

I walked forward, breaking the grip she had on my shoulder and back. "No, it's nothing."

"Okay, if you say so," she said in a soft, caring voice. "I'm gonna go collect some water from the lake to rinse off with. Hopefully I can cool it down enough."

I replied: "Okay."

The princess began to walk away.

Sigh...

A little pebble started to bounce around at the edge of my foot. *What the...?*

It was subtle, but the ground beneath my feet had begun to shake. A cold shiver shot down my spine. The ground began to crack in two.

A huge wave of heat blasted the back of my head, causing the

172

hair on my body to drip with sweat. All the grass in the surrounding area began to burn.

I could hear the sound of the earth crumbling, followed by water pouring down.

I heard a high pitched scream coming from behind me. "Keiko!"

I turned my head ever so slowly. My glance followed the sound of the pouring water, upwards into the sky. I lost my breath at the sight.

"Oh... my... god."

Chapter 13
Two Winged Beast

Dragons; magical creatures, presumed to be dead for hundreds of years. The reasoning behind how they accumulated so much power is extraordinary—back during the great war, the goblins and the elves came together in a desperate attempt to stop the humans from wiping them off the face of Geatree.

Various non-magical humans were infused with both elf and goblin magic. The elves used dark magic to corrupt the souls of the humans they captured. Once a human's soul was fully corrupted, they were handed over to the goblins for further experimentation. The goblins took advantage of the adaptability in human DNA. They used morphing magic to warp their DNA and merge it with various other creatures. They were often unsuccessful, and many humans were subjected to their failed experiments.

Their eyes were torn from their sockets, and their teeth were ripped from their gums. Their bones were bent from out of their backs and forced into the shape of wings. Legends said that the screams of those being experimented on could be heard from miles away. The humans who survived the various bone rear-rangements were then injected with numerous magical serums every hour on the hour for months.

Their blood started to change color, and scales started to peek on the surface of their skin. The bones sticking out of their backs started to grow painfully larger. They would scream, and scream, and scream… but no one ever came to help.

Colored orbs began to sprout from thin stems in their empty eye sockets. The goblins force-fed them gorwa fruit, a fruit that caused uncontrollable rage. Their tempers shortened, and their anger grew. Numerous subjects died during the testing stage, and only a few survived.

Many months passed before they finally had a breakthrough: after a good deal of trial and error, the goblins were finally able to create prototypes of their new beast.

The creatures cried in agony all day long from the pain of their transformation. The elves saw the size of the creatures and despised their resemblance to the humans. They took the few surviving prototypes and moved them down south to Lindia, the kingdom of the elves.

There, these nameless creatures were escorted to the tree of life, where they were pumped full of magic that stemmed directly from the core of Geatree. Their bodies grew in size, and their limbs altered in shape, until they were proportional to the size of the creatures' bodies. Their teeth straightened, and the broken wings on their backs grew a hundred times in size. The pain of their existence was lifted off their shoulders. Their tail bones began to stretch to massive lengths and grew thick skin around them.

The elves used their beautifying magic to enhance the creatures' colored patches of skin until the color consumed the entirety of their body surface. The newly formed creatures' skin began to radiate from all the magic seeping into them. They were beautiful, they were powerful, they were enormous, they were born from the broken souls of humans, they were—dragons. These creatures were thought to be so perfect that they received the divine blessing of the gods, turning them into holy creatures, and now one happened to be standing before Keiko and the princess.

Moments ago, the three suns had been hanging halfway above the horizon in the evening sky, shining just bright enough to caress the edges of my eyes, but that was no longer the case.

Now I was unable to see anything. Black smoke and burning ash blocked out the rays of light from the three suns. The Lake of Wonders, once a beautiful place where I had memories of spending time with my Grandpa, was now a fiery pit of lava. The green grass surrounding the lake had vanished in an instant; all that was left behind was burnt earth.

I'd caught a glimpse of the beast exiting the lake just before the sky turned black. There was no doubt in my mind that this was the dragon Lola had spoken about. I couldn't see them, but I could hear the dragon's massive wings whooshing down on the air, high in the atmosphere.

Foomp... Foomp... Foomp...

My body sat still—all I did was listen. The dragon let off a deep, menacing roar. *It was here all along.*

I heard a voice far to my right.

"Tempest! Ignite! Infuse!"

What?

The princess had just cast three spells. Her long golden hair was being swept away in the frantic winds surrounding her body. The power of the combat spell fused with her shiny blue dagger, creating a sharp water-vapor blade that exploded on impact, and she was no longer covered in the shapeshifter's disgusting sludge.

The expression on her face screamed, "Bring it on." She looked very, very angry. This was the first time that I had seen her this way. I was frightened. *Is that really the princess over there?*

She wasted no time. She bent her knees and launched herself into the dark, eerie sky. Ashes were flung from the center of the smoke she had burst through.

Bolts of blue light flashed behind the dark clouds, followed by an explosive sound. I could hear the princess's voice as she slashed away at the thick scales on the dragon's back.

Just as I was about to move, a beam of fire shot through the clouds in my direction.

"Wahhh!"

I jumped out of the way just in time. The ground where I'd been standing was no longer there.

My chest tightened, and my lungs started to fail from inhaling the burning ash. I coughed and coughed. *I can't stop coughing. I need to get above the smoke.*

I conjured up a tempest spell, and followed the princess's path up towards the dragon. The wind brushed down past my body. *How far up did she go?*

Burnt ash flew into my eyes. I clenched them tight and shouted a spell. "Yamadasi!"

'Yamadasi' is a spell that temporarily removes any feeling from the user's body. Because I'd used 'yamadasi,' my eyes were now pain free, allowing me to reopen them.

The moment I opened my eyes I noticed that I was above the

smoke, where I was greeted by the sight of the glorious beast. It was huge, easily spanning over five hundred feet in length. The brightness of the three suns reflected off its sharp crimson scales, and the claws on its feet were triple my height.

The dragon's body seemed to flow in a fluid motion, almost like a large whale swimming through the evening sky. My eyes locked on to the bright orange orbs in its eye sockets—they were mesmerizing. It was truly beautiful.

A human turned into a beast, said to have been enhanced by the elves and blessed by the gods. Not even I could have guessed that it would look this beautiful.

Suddenly, the princess appeared from the dark clouds below. "Ahhhhhhh!"

She slashed at the creature's back, leaving nothing but a scratch. The dragon grew angry, and began to fly at a greater speed.

"I have to help her!" Our goal was to slay this dragon and return to Lola with samples of its blood.

I wasted no more time. The evening was fading into night, so 'golden scythe' would not be efficient. I decided to use 'darkened scythe' instead. The moon was just peaking over the edge of the horizon. The spell would start off weak, but over time it should grow in power.

"Darkened scythe!" The moon's light rays warped around the edges of my fingers, creating black, curved claws. It had been a long day, and I had fought many creatures. My magical energy was low, but I knew that if I infused my 'darkened scythe' spell with the princess's combat-infused dagger, I would be able to kill this thing.

The corners of my lips creased up towards the edges of my cheeks, revealing to the world my glossy white smile. "Let's do this!"

I kicked off the strong winds surrounding my body and blasted towards the enormous dragon.

"Ahhhhh!" I slammed my black claws into the crimson scales under its eyes.

It let out a deep roar. "Rrrrrrrrrrr!"

"Die!" I shouted.

My heart was pounding and I could feel an adrenaline rush. This was the feeling I knew and loved so much. My arms swung furiously.

My smile widened after every slash. My tongue licked the crusted edges of my lips. I was loving every moment of this. "Hahahahah!"

"Tempest! Tempest! Tempest!"

I increased my speed while swarming around the dragon. I was leaving slash marks all over its body.

"This is great!"

"Keiko—watch out!"

"Huh?" I looked at the princess in confusion. Only then did I notice the dragon's wing coming directly for me. The large limb blocked out the light of the moon, causing my 'darkened scythe' spell to weaken, until it vanished completely.

"Oh... shit."

Whack!

"Blahhh!"

The force of the dragon's wing impacting my body caused blood to shoot out of my mouth. My tempest spell had also been stopped from the sheer force of the dragon's blow. I was now falling downwards at an unstoppable speed.

My head was pounding, and I was rapidly growing dizzy. It was then that I noticed a shining blue light headed straight for me.

The heat coming from the light was intense, and only strengthened as it got closer. *Am I going to die?*

I got carried away in the heat of the moment. A single tear fell from my right eye, making its way to the bottom of my cheek before evaporating off my face. "Damn."

"Keiko!"

The princess's voice. How lovely.

I felt a strange sensation lifting in my body, and that was the last thing I felt before blacking out.

Princess Valentinas point of view -

Twenty Seconds Earlier:

My lungs were struggling as I was furiously attacking the dragon with everything I had. There were multiple villages nearby, and as *the princess* of the Zaria Kingdom, I couldn't risk letting it get too close to them.

Huh? Is that Keiko? "Keiko, watch out!"

My body froze in fear as I watched the dragon smash its wing down on Keiko's head. "This is bad!"

I had to help him, but I wasn't close enough. Even if I increased the speed of my tempest spell, I wouldn't be able to make it there in time. *What can I do?*

Keiko was falling rapidly. The dragon hunched its back and opened its mouth wide. Saliva was dripping from the trenches in its gums. The inside of its mouth was rigid and black.

What's that?

The dragon's throat began to emit a bright blue light. My eyes widened at the realization of what was about to happen next.

I shouted his name as loud as I could with the hope that he would hear me and somehow move out of the way. "Keiko!"

"Rrrrrrrrrrr"

It was too late, the dragon had exhaled a massive beam of magic. I panicked and my palms started sweating, causing the handle of my dagger to get wet. If it weren't for that sensation, I would have never have thought of what I was about to do next.

"Infuse!"

I infused my 'tempest' spell into my dagger. The result of the spell was a combat-tempest weapon. Because I'd infused my 'tempest' spell, it no longer surrounded my body. Therefore I began to plummet to the ground.

The blue magical beam was seconds away from striking Keiko. My hair was blowing into my face, making it almost impossible to see. I pulled back my dagger and aimed it at the dog tag around Keiko's neck, and with all my strength, I threw it.

Black smoke shrouded my body as I re-entered the smoke and ash-filled atmosphere that the dragon had created.

"Please—Akemi, goddess of life and prosperity, save him!"

187

Princess Valentina was completely surrounded by black smoke, leaving her unable to see the result of her throw.

The dagger flew through the air in Keiko's direction. The sharp tip of the blade was headed straight for the top of Keiko's necklace. At the same time, the beam of light grew closer to the boy.

The dagger was slightly above the necklace, and just as it was about to miss, a golden aura encased Keiko's body, lifting him up ever so slightly.

Ding!

The dagger entered the circle of Keiko's necklace, catching onto the edge of the shiny silver chain and dragging him to the side, but not before he was hit by the dragon's attack.

No physical harm was done to him, but he was now unconscious.

The dagger flew down towards the ground, not stopping until the sharp edge of its blade penetrated a large purple stone that had been forged by the dragon's awakening.

The combat spell infused into the dagger erupted, allowing for easy access into the thick rock.

***

Luckily, I had landed in a bush. Although the leaves and branches cushioned my fall, the sharp sticks and thorns left scratches all over my body.

"Please Keiko… stay alive."

Chapter 14
A Princess's Love

Princess Valentinas point of view -

My body was hurting, and I had no idea where Keiko was. *My adventurer rank is supposed to be M-SSS and I can't even stick a landing. How can this be?*

I did my best to exit the bush as swiftly as possible. Thorns were poking me across my entire body, and sticks along with various twigs and leaves were tangled in my hair.

"Stupid twigs, get out!" I shouted.

I ripped the twigs and leaves from my hair and brushed the dirt off my arms. The three suns had fully set and the moon was out in full view. The sky was dark, and the black smoke was no help. I couldn't see a single thing.

"I hope Keiko is okay. I have to find where he landed. It has to be nearby."

I was aware of a foreign feeling in my chest. My face was sweaty and my heart felt damaged. *What is this feeling? Is it because I'm worried about him?*

A couple of quiet seconds passed, before a loud echoing roar could be heard from above the clouds.

"I am not weak—I will not give in to the likes of you."

Between the minotaur, headless man, and the shapeshifting girl, Keiko and I had gone through far too much pain and suffering to just give up now.

"Ouch!" A drop of fiery lava splashed onto my leg. I quickly blew it away with a tempest spell.

I took a deep breath, allowing the hot ashy air to enter my lungs. It hurt, and I began to cough. *I guess slowing down my breathing to remain calm is out of the question.*

I didn't have my dagger, so I was now forced to rely on only my magic if I wanted to attack the dragon again. I had never seen a dragon in the flesh before, let alone many other mythical beasts. Father had kept me sheltered my entire life. *I'll show him.*

I looked at the surrounding area for any small rocks that weren't blazing hot. "This will do."

I did my best to quickly collect as many as I could. *If I can keep the dragon distracted while I search for Keiko, then I don't have to worry about it flying off and attacking any nearby villages.*

Just thinking about him made my heart skip a few beats. I

could feel the blood rushing to my face. *Why do I get so hot and nervous every time I think about him?*

I slapped myself in the face twice, sharply. "This isn't the time for silly questions, I have to hurry up!"

I darted towards the forest with the rocks in my hands. If I was correct, and my dagger had been able to save Keiko, then he should have landed somewhere in the forest. Finding him was the best way for me to stop this dragon.

As I ran towards the forest, I felt an eerie presence appearing above me.

Foomp...

Foomp...

Foomp...

The dragon's huge muscular wings sliced through the air with ease, causing an enormous downdraft to smash into my back. I was almost to the tree line, and even though I was directly underneath the dragon it hadn't noticed me yet.

"Huff... huff... huff!"

I was exhausted, but I wasn't ready to give up. I had no choice, there were innocent villages nearby, and it was my duty as the princess to ensure their safety.

Just this morning the area surrounding the forest had been a giant open field, full of life and beauty, but now it was different. The ground, once soft and lush, was covered in large purple rocks, and all the grass had been burnt off the surface of the soil.

I cautiously jumped over little rivers of lava running through the cracks in the surface. My boots splashed in puddles, causing lava to fling everywhere. Luckily, I was able to avoid it.

"There it is!" I had made it to the entrance of the forest, and I wasted no time entering it. I had a plan, but I needed to find some materials first.

Boom!

A sudden blast of magic caused me to fly forwards into the dirt, as I did, all the rocks were flung from my hands. "Wahhh!"

My knees dug deep into the hard, solid terrain, and my chest smashed into the nearest tree. All the air in my lungs was ripped right out by the force of the impact.

"Huff… huff… huff…"

"What was that?" I looked up at the sky and was greeted by a frightening sight. The crimson dragon was lighting the forest on fire. *Its power is unreal.*

Like all the other magical creatures of Geatree, dragons too, had a smell. Ever since it had awoken, my senses had gone crazy. My nose was clogged with the smell of mana, and my ears were ringing from the countless spells that had been cast by Keiko and me.

I gathered up all the purple rocks again and took off deeper into the forest. "There has to be something around here."

I darted through the forest as fast as I could looking for anything that could be bent without breaking. A couple minutes went by before I finally stumbled upon something useful.

"This is perfect!"

Hidden under the earth, covered by dirt and mud, was a set of rubber adventurer gloves. I began to tear the gloves in half. I then ripped the laces out of my boots. I took the four half-gloves and rolled them into thin rubber rectangles.

"I hope this works!"

I took my shoe laces and wrapped them around the rubber gloves, making sure they were tight and sturdy. I then reached to my left and grabbed the largest branch that I could find hanging from a tree.

I grabbed the loose branch and tugged it until it snapped free from the tree trunk. Everything was coming together just as I hoped for. I took the rubber fixture I had made and tied one end to the top of the branch, and the other to the bottom of it.

Once the rubber fixture was tightly fastened to the branch, I rushed back over to the pile of rocks sitting on the ground.

I knelt down and held my hands out over the rock pile. "Acies!" I shouted.

'Acies' is a spell that allows the user to create sharp edges from smooth surfaces. It was perfect for my current plan.

The rocks began to levitate, and as they did so, little shards started to break off. Eventually, the smooth original structure of the rocks had turned into sharp jagged edges.

"Yes, yes, yes!" I shouted.

I heard the dragon roar once again, and the blaze he'd lit among the trees started to make its way towards me. I could feel the heat of the fire warming up my body with every passing second. The intensity of the flames caused me to sweat from head to toe.

Once the rocks had all been sharpened, I cast an elevation spell on the makeshift bow I had made from the branch and the rubber gloves. I then shot one rock in the dragon's direction. Whilst doing so, I made sure to cast a mimicking spell onto the bow. Just as I'd planned, the bow was now firing sharp rock shards at the dragon all on its own.

"Yes! It worked."

The feeling of joy filled my body. I began to jump up and down.

"I did it, I did it, I got the dragon's attention. I did it, I did it, I got the dragon's att…"

Then it hit me. I had gotten the dragon's attention, and was standing next to the bow dancing. I quickly turned pale at the sight of the dragon charging down at the bow.

"Tempest!" I blasted a magical whirlwind towards the bow, right as the dragon was about to destroy it. The tempest spell carried the bow around the forest in random movements, making it hard for the dragon to destroy it.

"Perfect, the dragon's distracted. Time to find Keiko."

The night was dark and I struggled to see anything. The density of the forest would make it hard to locate Keiko. I thought about flying up into the sky with a tempest spell, but then the forest canopy would block my view of the ground below.

The only reasonable thing I could think of was to use 'darkened scythe.' The black curved claws around my fingers would have some illumination to them. It wouldn't be a lot, but at least it would be something.

I took advantage of the spell and slashed through any trees or foliage in my way. The sound of rocks whistling through the air pierced my ears.

"Good, the spell is still in effect."

I have no way of telling which direction I'm running in. I could use 'tempest' to fly up, but that spell always drains a lot of my magical energy. I could always use 'ignite.'

I planted the heels of my boots into the dirt. I veered to my left.

"This will do."

I picked up a small lizard that had been resting on a branch nearby. "Sorry little buddy!"

I lowered my hand down past my knees, then squatted to the floor. *Please forgive me!*

"Hiyyyaaahh!" I heaved myself upwards, lifting my arm. In doing so, I released the lizard from my hand and flung it in the air.

"Ignite!" Instantly, a water-vapor arrow appeared from thin air and catapulted itself towards the lizard.

Boom!

The explosion caused a massive gust of wind to force the smoke and ash out of the area. The force of the wind was greater than any spell I could have conjured up.

I was now able to see the open sky with zero obstacles in my way. I noticed that the dragon was growing absolutely furious. *There can't be that many rocks left. I have to find Keiko so we can kill this thing together!*

I had tossed the dagger towards Keiko in the direction of the setting suns. I noticed that the moon was on my right, so Keiko had to be somewhere to my left.

I took off deeper into the forest. Eventually, I stumbled upon large purple boulders that resembled the rocks I had picked up.

"What the heck is this... huh? Keiko!"

My eyes widened at the sight. Keiko was alive and hanging from a boulder. The foreign feeling in my chest vanished without a trace. A small tear bubbled up in the corner of my eye. It truly was a miracle.

I rushed to the top of the boulder. The ground was quaking as a result of the dragon's explosions.

"Keiko, Keiko... wake up!"

I started to lightly slap Keiko's face. "Wake up! I need you here with me. Please!"

All hope of fighting off the dragon began to leave me. Sure, I knew I was strong, and capable of using magic, but the dragon was a creature with abilities said to be gifted from the gods. I alone was no match for it.

I realized at that moment how naive I had been. I'd forced Keiko to come with me on this quest and he was now paying for it. His body was bruised, and his hands were covered in dirt.

I eased myself up while holding onto Keiko's jacket and grabbed the dagger. I tugged backwards with all my might until it finally broke loose from the giant purple stone.

"Wahhhh… oof! Ahh. That hurt." The dagger had been the only thing holding us against the rock.

I slowly sat up and placed my hand on the back of my head. My fingers felt wet. I brought them back around and looked at them, and to my surprise there was blood all over my hand.

"I guess I could have thought that through a bit better."

I brushed myself off and stood up. Then I put my arms under Keiko's shoulders and dragged him away from the rocks and towards a nearby tree. Upon arrival, I leaned him against the base of the tree and brushed back his hair.

His hair felt soft, like a puppy's fur. My heart was racing and my body felt excessively warm. I crawled closer to him, wrapping my legs around his.

I couldn't wake him up through any normal means, so there was only one thing left to try. I placed my hands on either side of his oddly soft yet rough face.

Every time I did what I was about to do, that foreign feeling entered my chest and I could feel my face flush. I didn't understand this feeling, but I could never tell him that. I wanted him to see me as strong and independent, but this sensation made me feel weak and vulnerable.

I leaned inwards, bringing my face closer to his, closing the gap between our lips. My lips were less than an inch away, and although they weren't touching his, I could feel a tingly sensation in them as they got closer.

Finally our lips touched—the feeling was nothing short of magical. Every time we kissed I could feel our bond growing stronger on a level that was inexplicable.

This feeling... is it perhaps... love?

My heart fluttered at the thought. I placed my hand on his chest, just above his heart. It, too, was fluttering.

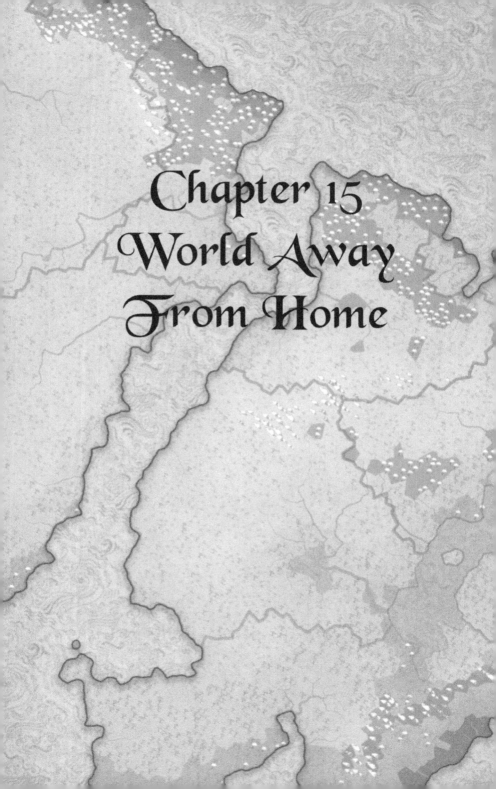

Chapter 15
World Away
From Home

"Babe! Wake up, you have to help me get the kids ready for school."

The ... kids?

"Daddy! Wake up, Daddy!"

"Wahhh!"

A sudden burst of love and laughter filled my body. My hands tingled with joy as two soft little heads nestled into my palms. *This is nice.*

My eyes opened slowly as the smell of warm bread and mashed potatoes covered in gravy entered my nostrils.

Sniff... sniff...

What a beautiful smell.

I awoke from my slumber to find two little children clinging onto me. Their soft little fingers were curled around my chest, and their faces were full of smiles and laughter.

"Daddy's awake!" said the little boy.

"Good morning, Daddy. Look, look! I helped Mommy make

you breakfast," said the boy's younger sister.

A soft, elegant voice called from across the way. "Luffy! Mio! Get off your father and get ready for school!

Father?

The little kids sighed and climbed down off my bed. I removed the warm heavy blanket from my legs, then swung them off the bed. *What are these clothes that I'm wearing?*

Oddly enough, I was already fully dressed. I was wearing a thin white shirt that allowed for the slight breezes to caress my body, and from the waist down a pair of light gray jeans.

Fuzzy blue socks wrapped my feet cozily. I felt relaxed and at ease, so much so that a sleepy yawn escaped my lips.

"Keiko, darling, are you coming to eat breakfast?" the soft voice asked.

I spoke without thinking: "Yeah, just a minute!"

I started to leave the comfort of my bed when a sudden pain shot through my forehead. "Ahhh!"

I placed my hand on my head in a desperate attempt to ease the throbbing pain. After a few short seconds, the pain faded away. *What was that?*

I looked towards the corner of the room. Next to the small stone fireplace was a pair of brown leather boots. The boots had thin black straps with shiny red buckles on them. I made my way over to the boots and picked them up. *Strange, why do I feel like I've seen these before?*

I shrugged off the feeling and eased my feet into the boots. The warm smell of delicious food found its way into my nose again. My mouth was watering and my stomach began to growl.

Mhmhmhmhmhm...

My stomach is growling like crazy. I must be hungry.

I followed the trail of the delicious smell down a long hallway. The floorboards were creaky and the lights were dull. At the end of the hallway was a large opening that appeared to be another room.

I walked through the opening. The three suns shone their rays of light into my eyes, giving me a boost of energy.

"Good morning, darling. Your breakfast is on the counter."

I glanced to my left, towards where the soft voice had come from. "Princess? Is that you?"

The blonde, womanly figure standing in front of me chuckled. "You haven't called me Princess in years, babe. What's gotten into you? Just call me Valentina, like you always have."

I stared at her. My head started to pound again. "Ahhhh." I put my hand to my forehead once more to ease the throbbing pain.

"What's wrong, honey? Come sit down and eat some breakfast—it'll make you feel better."

Valentina set her perfect little hands on my back and assisted me to the table. Then she pulled out a chair and sat me down.

"Daddy, what's wrong?" asked the young boy.

"Daddy, are you okay?" asked the young girl.

I looked at the two children. Their little red ears were perked up in curiosity. I could tell they were sincerely worried for me.

"Yeah… I'm fine." I said.

I was just as confused as they were. I had no memories of any past events; the only thing I could remember was an odd dream

I'd just had.

"Eat up, love. Mio helped me cook this meal just for you."

I looked over at the little girl. Her hands were clasped together and her eyes were shimmering with excitement.

I picked up the steel fork at my place setting. It was cold to the touch. "Wow, this smells really good."

I dug my fork deep into the warm mashed potatoes piled on my plate. My mouth was watering even more from the delicious smell.

"Don't forget the gravy, darling."

Gravy?

Before I knew it, Valentina was pouring thick creamy gravy onto my potatoes. It only increased my desire to eat. I began to wolf down the potatoes, along with some of the warm bread. The outside of the bread was hard and crispy, but the inside was soft and delicate.

"Mio! This is really good. It tastes amazing."

Mio's smile widened and her ruby eyes lit up with joy. "Yay!"

"Alright kids, time for school. Get your bags and head on out."

"Okay," they said simultaneously.

The children rushed to grab their things and dashed out the front door into the village streets.

Valentina sat down in the chair next to mine and joined me for breakfast. She gently brushed her hair back behind her ear as she ate her mashed potatoes. *Wow, she really is beautiful.*

"Is your head feeling okay, darling?"

"Yeah, it feels fine now. I just had a weird dream, and maybe that's the cause."

"A dream? What about, love?"

She turned towards me, locking her gaze on mine. I could tell by the way she was looking at me that she was genuinely interested in hearing what I had to say.

I began to explain my dream: "We were young, about seventeen, almost eighteen, I would say. For some reason that I can't remember, we were fighting a dragon."

"A dragon? How crazy—dragons don't exist," she said, laughing.

"Hey, now. Like I said, this was just a dream."

"Okay, okay. Please continue your story, my love."

"Like I was saying, we were fighting a dragon and for some reason I was falling from the sky. You were flying around the dragon really fast, slashing at it and trying to kill it."

"Me, kill a dragon? I wouldn't hurt a soul."

"I know, I know. Anyway, the last thing I remember seeing was the starry night sky, followed by a huge beam of light."

Valentina laughed. At that moment, I felt a warm feeling in the center of my chest. *This is nice.*

Hmm... I could really go for some water right about now.

"Tempest." I waited for a moment but nothing happened.

"Tempest." *Still nothing?*

"What are you doing?" Valentina asked.

"Casting a 'tempest' spell to carry that cup of water over here."

The look on her face showed her complete confusion.

"Tempest spell? Are we in a fantasy world?"

Oh yeah, that's right. Magic doesn't exist, so why did I try to cast a spell?

Valentina looked me in the eyes. I think she could tell that I was puzzled.

"You should go outside and get some fresh air," she said.

"Yeah, I think I'll do that." I got up from the kitchen table and walked towards the door that the kids had just gone through. As I did so, I came to the realization that I had no idea where I was.

What is this place? How long have we been here?

I didn't recognize a single person, tree or animal. My eyes began to pulse with pain. "Ahhh."

"Hey, Valentina!"

"What is it, Keiko?"

"How long have we been living here?"

"Hmm. Well, my father gifted us this house right before Luffy

212

was born, so about eight years."

Eight years! My son is eight years old? Why can't I recall a single thing about him then?

I had no memories of my children, moving into my house, or even marrying my wife. "Hey, where is the closest Adventurers' Guild?"

"Uh... just walk further into town, and make a right past the fountain. Don't you know? I mean, you do work for them as an adventurer, after all."

"Right—I'll be on my way, then." I left home and headed for the guild. As I was doing so, Valentina pulled me aside and gave me a kiss. Our lips were sealed for a few short moments, then I was on my way.

That kiss felt... strange. Something is wrong.

"Maybe I'll ask Lola if she knows what's going on. Wait... who is Lola, and why did I just say her name?"

I made my way to the center of town and eventually came across the fountain. *Where have I seen this before?*

"Ahhh!" A sudden sharp pain shot through my head. This time the pain was even more intense than before. I dropped to my knees and grabbed my temples.

Random images of blood and gore were shooting through my mind. There was blood everywhere, and I could hear the screams of a little girl crying for help. Blue, bubbly figures were sloshing around in my mind. I started to scream from the pain that the images brought with them.

"Sir... sir! Are you okay?"

"Huh?"

I glanced upwards. As I did so, the painful thoughts left my mind. The person standing in front of me had a familiar face.

"Lola, it's you! Please, something strange has been going on and I need you to help me figure out what it is!"

"Uhm... sir, who are you?"

"I'm..." *Wait, who am I? I heard Valentina call me Keiko, but is that my name?*

"It's me, Keiko!" It was then that it hit me. *Have I ever met this girl before? Why do I know her name?*

"Uhm, sir, how do you know my name?"

I was just thinking that!

"I... I don't know."

"Let me help you up."

Lola bent down and grabbed me under the arms. She then pulled me up and helped me regain my balance.

"Can you escort me to the Adventurers Guild, please?" I asked.

She smiled. "Of course I can!" *What a friendly soul.*

Upon arriving at the adventurers guild, I ran into a not-so-familiar face.

"Keiko! Hey buddy, what's up?"

Huh? Who is this guy?

Before me stood an average sized man. He had a sword attached to his hip and a sash full of brightly colored liquids.

"Who is this lovely lady?" he asked.

"This is my friend, Lola."

"Well, we just met, but yes—I would consider us friends, too," she said.

The man leaned in towards my ear and whispered, "Yo, is this your mistress?"

I jumped back in shock. "What? No, I don't have a damn mistress! She's just a friend."

"So, what I'm hearing is that she's single?," he said.

"Hello! This single girl can hear you, you know."

The man's face flushed blood-red. "My apologies, my lady. My name is Ryan. I am Keiko's adventuring partner."

So that's who he is. What does he mean by an adventuring partner? Do we have some kind of party?

Lola and Ryan seemed to be off to a nice start. I looked at the two of them casually flirting when suddenly the same sharp pain began to throb in my head once more.

"Ahhh!" I fell to the ground.

"Oh my god, are you alright, Keiko?" asked Lola.

Ryan shouted: "Keiko!"

"Yeah... I'm okay, guys."

I regained my balance and stood up. Seeing the two of them flirting made me think of my past with Valentina, except there was no past. I couldn't remember a single thing. *What is going on with me?*

"Hey Lola, you should join our adventuring party. It would be totally fun. Keiko and I get a little lonely sometimes. Haha," Ryan said, while rubbing the back of his neck.

I agreed with Ryan's statement, and Lola seemed to like the idea.

"Alright, now that's settled, why don't we take you to get your rank, Lola?"

I totally forgot about the ranking system! Now that I'm thinking about it, doesn't it involve a gargoyle or something?

"Alright, Ryan. Where is the room with the gargoyle?"

The two stood there looking at me in utter confusion, only to burst out laughing shortly after.

"Keiko, you are such a funny man," Ryan said.

"What he said." Lola agreed.

"That was a good laugh you gave us. Okay, Lola, let's go to the counter and get you an assessment."

Did I say something funny?

I shrugged it off. We walked over to the counter. Sitting behind the desk was an exact copy of Lola, the only difference being her eyes. This woman had bright green eyes. The way they dressed, looked, and even spoke were oddly similar.

"Hey sister!" said the lady behind the desk.

That explains it.

"Hey Alol!" Lola said with a big smile.

Alol... Isn't that just Lola backwards? What the heck?

After filling out about fifty forms, Lola was given an adventurer ranking class of "M-D."

"Class M, so there is magic in this world?" I said.

"What are you talking about, silly? The 'M' on the adventurer card stands for mighty, as in Mighty's Adventurers' Guild. The place where we are standing right now!" Ryan said.

Why did I think "M" stood for magic? Well, whatever.

"Okay, guys, what's our first mission going to be?" I asked.

"Why don't we go see what's posted on the board?" Lola said.

We all walked over to a wooden board on the wall. There were about thirty sheets with quests listed on them, hanging from pins. I shuffled through them all and found nothing about any magical beast.

"How about this one, Keiko?" Ryan said.

I grabbed the sheet from his hand. It read:

Black-armored Knight. Wanted for the destruction of a local town. Reward - 70,000 Yupps.

"Seventy-thousand yupps! Wait, what's a yupp?" I asked.

The yupp is a form of currency in Geatree. A single yupp corresponds to one USD, or approximately one hundred ten Yen.

Lola leaned towards Ryan. "Is this guy crazy?" she asked.

"Alright—enough laughing, you guys. Let's just start this quest," I said.

Lola, Ryan and I set off on our very first quest as a fully-established adventuring crew. We made our way through the local forest and to a large lake sitting at the center of an open field.

This field, this lake… it… it… nah, it doesn't ring any bells. We carried on.

We crossed the lake on a small wooden boat that happened to be conveniently floating nearby. We were headed for the village that the knight had destroyed. Eventually, we could see smoke in the distance.

"We must be close," I said.

We managed to make it to the village in a timely fashion.

"There he is!" Ryan shouted.

First the boat was so conveniently placed, now the knight is still here in the village, even though the request was posted three days ago. What is going on?

The three of us charged the knight. It wasn't until that moment that I realized how screwed I was. Ryan was the only one of us wearing shiny silver armor. Lola was dressed in protective battle gear, such as arm and knee pads. Both of them had some sort of weapon, but I was dressed in a normal shirt and pants, and as for weapons, I had none.

"Ah, crap!" I said.

The knight saw us charging him. I couldn't help but notice his shiny black armor. It looked familiar, but I couldn't figure out where I had seen it before. The knight was muscular and strong. His rich golden locks blew in the breeze so elegantly as he continued to stab children and burn down the village.

"What a beautiful man," I said.

What the hell am I saying?

Ryan and Lola rushed in towards the knight, but before they could attack him, he shoved his fingers into his mouth and whistled.

In an instant, an oversized bull emerged from the fire and rubble of the village. The bull had black fur and a thick silver ring in its nose. My eyes widened at the sight and I dropped to the ground once more with an aching pain in my head.

"Ahhhh!" *Why does this keep happening to me?*

I regained my senses and stood up. My body was trembling and I had an odd sensation of familiarity.

"Keiko, look out!" Ryan shouted.

I quickly moved out of the way, dodging what would have been a massive blow from the bull's horns just in time. The knight was now riding the bull, the two paired together to create a single impressive enemy.

I swiftly grabbed the sword from Ryan, and took a few colored balls from his sash.

"I don't know what these colored balls do, but I'm going to stop you from harming any more innocent villagers!"

Innocent villagers?

For a second time, a huge number of bloody images ran through my mind. Girls screaming, my ears being torn off, blood flying everywhere, and healing myself on a daily basis. The pain of the images in my head was unbearable. I had no choice left but to scream and hope for the best.

"Ahhhhhh!" I threw the orange colored ball at the ground near the bull's hooves.

Poof!

A ball of orange dust shot up into the atmosphere.

"Ack!" I started to cough frantically. "Ryan, what the hell is this shit?"

"Those are the colored balls for the gender reveal party my wife is having later."

I looked at him with a confused look on my face. "What gender is orange?" I asked.

"You know, silly—blue for boy, pink for girl, orange for demi-human boy, and red for demihuman girl."

"Guys! Is this really the time to be talking about this?" Lola shouted. "Wait… Ryan, you're married?!"

"Back to this guy," I said.

Looking at his armor I could tell it would be hard to hack through it. *The best option I have is to take off his head.*

I charged the bull-riding knight, screaming at the top of my lungs. "Ahhhhhhh!"

Ching!

Ching!

Ching!

The metal edge of Ryan's sword clashed against the knight's thick armor as he covered his face with his arm. "Come on guy, just die already! I don't have time for this. I have to figure out why I have this familiar feeling."

I ran past the bull, placing my foot on its thick metal nose ring, then jumping up with all my might. I was now in the air, about fifteen feet up. I was staring down at the knight. He said nothing.

This is it, this is my chance.

I positioned my sword downwards towards the top of his head. Just as my strike was about to land, he changed... and I froze.

I was now staring directly into the eyes of my daughter Mio. I was no longer on the battlefield, I was now home. *What is happening?*

"Babe! Wake up, you have to help me get the kids ready for school."

I started to freak out. Things were too similar to before. The kid's heads were in my palms, the breakfast that Mio and Valentina had made was on the counter in the same spot as it was before. The kids were running late for school, and my boots were in the same spot, next to the stone fireplace.

I quickly ran to the bathroom. Once inside, I started washing my face with water. *What is happening?*

I glanced up into the mirror, and that's when it hit me—hundreds of images began to cycle through my brain. The princess, the minotaur, the headless knight, the use of magic, the death of a nameless demihuman fox girl, the shapeshifters, and even the dragon!

I lost my breath as the thoughts crossed my mind. "Ahhhhh!"

"Darling, are you okay?"

I looked up into the mirror and regained my breath. I couldn't help but freak out a bit. "Sta… stay away from me!"

"What's the matter?"

I burst through the front door and made a dash for the center of the village. As I ran, the sky started to darken and an eerie sensation filled my body. All the villagers in the town started to look at me oddly. Their eyes started to glow and turn red, and their smiles quickly turned into frowns.

My heart began to race and my breathing rapidly picked up. I looked behind me, only to see that my children, along with Valentina, were chasing me. Their eyes also glowed red, and they had long knives in their hands.

Luffy leaped into the air, landing on my back. His tongue was hanging down past his chin, and drool was dripping everywhere. I shook him off and got back up. *This is insane!*

"Ack!"

Suddenly I couldn't move. Valentina was standing in front of me, and in her hand was that same long knife. And that knife… was in my gut.

I started to cough up blood. I could feel it dripping down my chin and onto my hands. My white shirt was stained red as blood poured out of my stomach.

Then, just as I was about to give up and accept my fate, I felt a strange warm feeling in the center of my chest. *Could it be?*

I reached into this glowing spot in my chest. *Thank you, princess, for sending me this gift.*

I grabbed onto the warm sturdy handle and pulled it outwards. Just as I'd expected, it was the katana forged from the bond of our two souls. *This is going to be fun!*

I lowered my head, locking my eyes with Valentina's. I smiled slightly and chuckled.

"You're not the real princess, and you never will be!"

I screamed, and as I did so, the handle of the katana transformed into a metal chain of about twenty feet in length. I started to spin the blade in a circle around me, and as a result, all the villagers' heads were chopped off, including my family's.

The headless bodies dropped to the floor. Small tears welled up in my eyes. I allowed one to escape before wiping it away. A bright green aura started to illuminate my entire body. My legs faded from existence.

Even though they had been a fake representation of my family, it made me sad to see them go. *I'm going to miss those little guys.*

My body was now almost fully faded into the green aura. "Don't worry, princess, I'll be back to you soon."

Chapter 16
Battle of Courage

A wet droplet of unknown essence rolled down the side of my face. It was warm. Something small was holding onto my shoulders. Its grip was tight, and it was holding me close. The sounds of fire and destruction echoed through the surrounding area, but a tingly sensation was beaming into my chest and onto my lips. *This feeling is so warm and so fuzzy. Could it be?*

Slowly, my eyelids broke their seal. When I opened them, my suspicions were confirmed. The princess had her legs between mine, and her hands were gripped on my shoulders. Tears were running down her cheeks and onto my own. Her thick blonde hair was gently blowing in the warm breeze.

The eruptions of fire and explosions had done nothing to affect her beauty. The amethyst crystals on her necklace highlighted her beautiful curves.

For the first time, I could say I truly felt something meaningful behind that kiss of hers. It didn't feel like a simple action used to strengthen her power. It felt… different. *Amazing.*

She pulled her lips away from mine. Her eyes were still shut, and the tears were flowing down her cheeks. I reached up and placed my right hand on her soft, innocent skin, and wiped the tears from off her face with my thumb.

I could tell a shock had gone through her body. She gasped. As she did so, her eyes bolted open and her lips started to quiver. More tears started to form at the edge of her eyelids. I looked directly into those lake-blue eyes.

"It's all right, princess. I'm back now."

I felt a small impact on my upper body.

"You... stupid dum-my! Why did y-you... charge in there s-s-so recklessly?" the princess asked.

She was crying harder than I had ever seen her cry before, to the point where she could barely speak. Her cheeks were flushed blood-red, and her face was swimming in tears.

"Princess... I—"

She charged at me, wrapping her arms around my body and embracing me tightly. She nuzzled up close. Her legs were between mine, and her head was resting on my chest. Her tiny little tears dropped from her face and onto my shirt. Her body was warm, and her arms felt so soft.

Although her hands and arms felt so pure and soft, her grip around my body was very tight. I could feel her shaking, as though she were scared.

"You… cou-could have died… y-you know! Then wh-what would I… do?"

I hadn't realized it until now, but my reckless actions had caused her a lot of pain. I'd been so focused on hurting the dragon that it hadn't occurred to me that I was also hurting the princess.

I wrapped my left arm around her back and set my right hand on top of her head. *The reason I was able to use the katana in that non-magical trance the dragon put me in was because of her kiss. It has to be.*

I stroked her hair. It was something I personally disliked because it made me feel like a dog, but looking at her face I could tell it brought her comfort.

"Princess, I'm so sorry. The last thing I wanted to do was make you worry, or leave you alone, and by being reckless I did both. I swear from this point on I won't rush onto the battlefield. Although, I do recall you were the first to attack the dragon."

She punched me in the stomach. "Shut up, dummy!"

We both laughed, and as we were laughing our eyes met. She looked magical; she was absolutely stunning. I wiped the remaining tears from her face with my hand. Then I brushed her hair back behind her ear, allowing me to see her perfect face. I felt a fuzzy feeling in my chest. She took my hand and placed it on her breast. I could tell she wanted me to feel her heart beating. It was beating fast, as was mine. I had an unknown feeling swelling up in the depths of my body. I leaned in towards her. She did likewise.

Our lips met.

The fuzzy feeling in my chest began to intensify. As her lips pulled away from mine, and our eyes opened, a bright light shone at the center of both our chests.

I reached into hers, and she reached into mine.

"Princess..."

"Keiko..."

I felt a large handle, but it was different from the katana. I pulled outwards, and she did too. A bright light flashed in our faces, causing us to move backwards. When the flash was gone, so too was the glowing light on our chests.

I felt something strange in my hand. I looked at it, only to see I was holding a large orange spear. The tip of the spear was glowing yellow, and so was the ribbon hanging from it.

I glanced at the princess. In her hand there was another spear, but hers was slightly different. The base of her spear was yellow, and the tip was glowing orange. She also had a glowing orange ribbon hanging from her spear.

"Hey, Keiko."

"What is it, princess?" I asked.

"What do you say we go slay this dragon and collect some blood samples?" She spoke with a smile of confidence on her face.

I chuckled. "Let's do this. We'll slay it together."

We tapped the edges of our spears together. The clink caused a small surge of magic to explode at their tips.

We looked at each other. It was easy to tell that we'd had the same idea. "Come on, princess, let's go kill that dragon!"

The dragon was flying in the direction of a local village. The princess and I wasted no time and made a rapid dash for the enclave. Luckily, due to a 'tempest' spell that I had cast, we were able to make it to the village before the dragon did. We ended up standing on top of a large stone clock tower, looking out at the huge beast heading our way.

The people of the village were running around in a panic. Although it was in the middle of the night and it was hard to see, there was nothing to block out the sight of the beast. Its large wings spanned one eighth of the village's size, and so it was quite noticeable.

Everybody was outside, lighting torches and gathering pitchforks. At first they'd been terrified, but when they'd seen the princess ready to fight it had encouraged them. The dragon was firing off random bursts of magic into the wilderness. Explosions and fires were coming into existence everywhere we looked. *If this dragon wants a fight, then I'm going to give him one!*

Back at the royal castle -

"Oh beautiful daughter of mine, how is your new maid doing?"

Oh? Is she not in her room?

"Oh, I see! They must be going for a midnight stroll. How beautiful—that girl is always doing her best for the kingdom. She deserves a rest."

I wonder if she's revealed her secret to that new maid yet? They are very similar, after all.

Back at the battlefield -

"Hey, princess, now that I think about it, what does your father think we're doing? You said that he locked your powers away, so I can't imagine he's okay with this."

"I don't know. He probably thinks we're taking a midnight stroll, or something."

"Hmm. Alright."

The best way to defeat the dragon would be to get the villagers involved. As this village was on a major trading route within the kingdom, it was quite large in size, so there were many people who could help. *It might be hard, but with the princess as the face of the fight, I think we can pull it off.*

The princess cast a projection spell. The only requirement for this spell was a simple chant. A large pink ring appeared in front of her mouth.

"Everybody listen up!"

Her voice was being transmitted to the entire town.

"Here's the plan…"

The princess went on to inform the villagers about our plan. As long as they were willing to help, we had a chance of taking the dragon down. As a means of persuading the villagers to aid us, we offered them the dragon's carcass. Creating rare stews, various weapons, and clothing out of the dragon's hide was sure to increase their economic state.

Ten minutes later -

"Everything seems to be in its proper place, princess."

"Good, now all we have to do is get the villagers excited," she said.

She turned towards me. "Keiko, I think you should ramp them up."

Me? Act as the representative of the kingdom?

"But princess, why me?" I asked.

"I believe you can do it, so give it a shot," she said.

I smiled. "Thank you, princess."

She once again cast a projection spell, this time in front of my mouth.

I must admit I was nervous. I had never spoken to a crowd this large before. I glanced over at the princess. She was smiling. *She has faith in me. I can't let her down!*

"Listen up, everybody. As you know, we have a seriously strong enemy approaching us. You have done a great job following the princess's instructions so far. Men! Fight for your wives, your children, and your desire to stay alive. Prove how strong you really are, and don't you dare let this worthless beast gain an ounce of satisfaction from destroying your homeland."

All the men in the crowd began to cheer. I felt a spark of joy inside me.

"Women! Fight for the fruit of your loins, your husbands, and your desire to live! Prove to that dragon that a woman can do it, too! Show that beast that It doesn't take a man's power to defeat it, and that a woman is just as strong! Show that oversized lizard that women bow down to no one!"

All the women in the crowd started to cheer really loudly. I might have been on the top of a clock tower, but that didn't stop their screams of joy from reaching my ears.

"Rise up above the odds and prove to the kingdom what you are worth! Earn those rewards and fight to stay alive!"

"Yeahhhh!" the crowd screamed.

"The princess and I are among you at this time, not for fun, but to aid you in the heat of battle, to serve you all, to shed our blood with the fallen, and to lay down our lives for the kingdom as well as the gods! We shall not be disgraced. We shall fight with honor!"

The crowd started to cheer louder than before. I couldn't help but smile. *A demihuman like me... being praised?*

A small tear fell from my eye. *I never thought I would see the day that people cheered for me.*

"Now... attack!" I shouted.

"Yeahhhhhhh!" the crowd screamed.

"What an excellent speech, Keiko. You would make a fine king, someday," said the princess.

I looked at her flushed face. She seemed to be sparkling in the moonlight. "What did you say?"

"Oh, nothing. Now come on, let's go fight."

The people of the village charged the dragon. They readied themselves with their bows and their other weapons. The few visible magic users were stationed on top of the stone wall surrounding the village. They had one job: to create a large shield over the enclave by combining their magic together. As instructed by the princess, a gap in their shield was left open just above where we were standing.

"Charrrrrge!" screamed the villagers as they ran into the heat of the battle.

The plan was for the princess to remain at the top of the clock tower while I charged the dragon with the villagers.

"Okay, princess, I'm going to help them now."

"Keiko, don't forget, as soon as the dragon makes its way over the barrier, you must come back here."

"Don't worry, princess, I'll make sure to come back to you this time."

She smiled. I did too.

I climbed down the clock tower and headed for the center of the battlefield. Adrenaline was pumping through my veins once more, and I felt a sudden rage overcome me. It was then that an image of the princess and the cheering villagers appeared in my head. *Remain calm, Keiko, for all of them.*

The feeling of rage ebbed away in my body. I was now back to my own stable mindset.

The dragon flew over the villagers, just as we'd planned. The hundreds of archers launched their most powerful arrows into the underside of the dragon's wings. Most of them failed to penetrate the dragon's tough skin, but many did.

Each arrow had a long, sturdy rope attached to the end of it with a small stake on the end. The dragon let out a massive roar as hundreds of arrows shot through the hide of its wings, and out the upper side. Its throat started to illuminate with a red glow. The dragon opened its mouth—it was charging up for a massive explosion. *Not on my watch, you filthy beast.*

"Now!" I shouted.

On my command, the hundreds of villagers whose arrows had penetrated the dragon pushed their stakes into the ground.

"Tonitura!"

I held my spear straight up into the sky above my head. A massive blue lightning bolt shot down from the clouds in the dark night sky. The colorful lightning lit up the battlefield.

The bolt struck the tip of my spear, causing a huge amount of magical energy to surge through it. I quickly spun the spear until it faced downward. I then lodged it into the ground.

"Ahhhhhhh!" I shouted.

The magical energy caused even my eyes to turn blue. The electric magic was being sucked from the sky and into the spear, through my body, and into the ground.

The power shot across the terrain I was standing on and into the stakes in the ground. It ran up the ropes attached to the stakes, and into the arrows. From there, the lightning magic spread out across the dragon's wings.

Boom!

A huge explosion on the dragon's wings caused it to stop attacking us. Instead it was plummeting towards the solid earth beneath it.

"Run!" I shouted.

The hundreds of brave men and women bolted back towards the safety of the village walls. As the dragon landed, some of them were crushed.

"Rrrrrrrrrrr!"

The dragon let out a screech of pain as it hit the ground.

I once again shouted the same words. "Now! Do it now!"

As the princess had planned, hundreds of villagers were stationed where we'd assumed the dragon would land. They were all equipped with matches, and each villager had been given a barrel full of black powder. On my command, the villagers lit their matches and tossed them onto the barrels.

The dragon began to pick itself up off the ground, when all of a sudden....

Boom!

...Boom!

...Boom!

...Boom!

...Boom!

Hundreds of explosive barrels exploded under and around the dragon's wings.

"Rrrrrrrrrr!"

The force of the massive explosions created holes in the dragon's wings; the blast setting them ablaze. The fire slowly started to peel away the thick skin from around its wings. The dragon slowly started to fly up from the ground.

As expected, the blast had not been enough to stop the sheer power of the dragon. But all we needed to do was weaken it. The dragon started to flap its wings, creating a huge gust of wind that put out the fire. The dragon was now bloody, and was just where we wanted it.

It locked its eyes onto the villagers who'd shot it with their arrows. They were now behind the walls of the village.

So far, so good. It's all going according to plan. It's time I made my way back to the princess.

I followed the dragon's path to the village. Once inside the walls, I used a tempest spell to quickly get back to the top of the clock tower.

"Princess, are you ready?" I asked.

"As ready as I'll ever be!" she replied.

The dragon started to charge itself up, firing off more explosive shots at the village. Thankfully, this village was on the verge of becoming a town, so the population was quite large, providing us with a fair amount of visible magic users to help us. The dragon fired off an attack. The beam of magic leaving its mouth bounced off the barrier.

The magic users screamed in agony as they struggled to keep hold of the barrier.

"You can do it! Don't give up!" I shouted.

The villagers were able to push back the dragon's attack. The creature was furious. It started to fire off a rapid number of attacks on the barrier. Its wings had been weakened, so it couldn't fly for very long. It had to land some time.

Just as we'd hoped, the dragon started to fly over the center of the village above me and the princess. It looked as though it was headed back towards the once peaceful, now lava-filled lake.

"Now!" the princess shouted.

On her command, half of the magic users holding up the barrier shifted their attention to the dragon. They converted their barrier magic to light magic.

"Darkened chains!" they shouted.

'Darkened chains' is the weaker version of its counterpart, 'golden chains.' 'Darkened chains' converts the light from the moon into a physical chain-like structure. The chains then move towards their target and wrap themselves around it. The spell can be broken, but it takes a massive amount of energy to do so.

Dozens of glowing black chains shot towards the dragon, wrapping themselves around its limbs and holding it in place.

I looked the princess in the eyes. "Here we go, princess."

We took the tips of our spears and lodged them into the clock tower, making sure that the two tips touched. As before, a surge of magic exploded out from the tips of the spears.

The magic burst ran up the clock tower and shot into the sky, directly above us. The blast went into the dragon's belly. The force of it was so strong that the princess and I could barely see. The wind forced us back, but we held onto the spears. If one of us were to let go, the blast would stop.

"Ahhhhhhh!" I yelled.

"Ahhhhhhh!" yelled the princess.

I can do it, I have to do it!

Boom!

A massive explosion happened at the center of the dragon's stomach.

"Rrrrrrrrrr!"

The dragon started to fall from the sky once again.

"Release the barrier and the chains!" I shouted.

The magic users followed my instruction, allowing the dragon to fall directly into the center of the village.

The three suns were starting to rise, but it was impossible to see. The dragon's body obscured every trace of the rising suns.

"Rrrrrrrrrr!"

In a desperate attempt to destroy the village, the dragon charged up for another attack, but it was too late.

Ching!

The dragon landed on top of the sharp clock tower. The pointed roof pierced right through its weakened hide. The dragon's purple blood splattered everywhere.

It was silent for a moment. I looked over at the princess's blood covered face, and she too looked at mine. A smile started to form on both our faces.

Almost as if it had been planned, the whole village was alongside me and the princess, and we were cheering.

"Yaaahhhhh!" we shouted.

I couldn't believe it. The princess's plan had worked. Excitement and joy ran through my body and before I knew it, I was hugging the princess. Tears of joy ran down my face.

"We did it, princess… we did it."

She embraced my body, hugging me back.

Back at the royal castle -

"Hey, Jiro," the king said, motioning to his butler.

"What is it, sire?" asked the butler.

"What was that large blast over yonder?" the king wanted to know.

"It was probably nothing, sire. I'm sure you're just seeing things."

"Yeah, you're probably right. Has the princess returned yet with her maid? They've been out for quite some time now."

"No, sire."

"Hmm, how strange. They must have stopped at a bakery on the way back. Oh, how my beautiful daughter loves sweets," the king said, smiling.

Back at the battlefield -

"How much do you wanna bet my father thinks we're getting sweets right now?" asked the princess.

We both started to laugh.

"Oh come on, give the man some credit. He's the king, he can't be that delusional," I said.

We both laughed again. *Wow. This feels amazing. Just the two of us, covered in blood and laughing all the way up here.*

"Alright, princess. Let's collect these long awaited blood samples and give them to Lola."

I removed the four vials from my sash and filled them with the dragon's blood. It was then that I heard a strange sound.

Woosh…

Huh? What was that?

A shadowy figure dashed past my face and grabbed the four vials from my hand. He was so fast that I didn't see it coming.

The figure leaped into the air, pausing in the middle of the three suns. It was hard to see his face, and he had on a long black cloak that covered most of his body. He turned his head ever so slightly.

I stood there in confusion. "Wait… is that?"

"It might just be," the princess said.

Chapter 17
Red Haired Foe

Keiko and the princess, along with the villagers, were successful in defeating the dragon. Although some villagers had died, by following the princess's plan they were able to keep casualties to a minimum. It was about time the two adventurers wrapped up this quest of theirs, but unfortunately an unfamiliar foe had appeared on the battlefield.

"Princess, are you thinking what I'm thinking?"

"Yeah, let's go!"

The cloaked figure took off through the streets of the village. The princess and I followed closely behind him.

Wow! His speed and agility are amazing.

I was running with all my strength. I had been up for two days, fighting all sorts of enemies. If I had to describe myself in one word right now it would be 'exhausted.'

The cloaked figure was running at an incredible speed, and his agility was amazing. I followed him through the streets of the village and into a tight alley between the church and the local bakery.

I was getting closer by the second, slowly but surely gaining on him. I had always been the one being chased, whether it was by the royal guards or some random goons whose stuff I'd just stolen; I had always been on the escaping side, but now I was the one trying to stop this figure from escaping.

It's funny how things can change so quickly. If it weren't for the princess, I would probably be running from her right now, and not be the one helping her.

Little by little I got closer to the cloaked figure.

I've got you now!

Or so I thought...

"Wahhhh!" I shouted.

The figure attempted to slow me down by tossing a wooden crate full of apples at my face. Sadly, it worked. I wasn't able to dodge the crate in time and ended up taking it right in the face.

"Oweeee!"

I was knocked backwards.

The princess was running with me. The only difference was that she was chasing him from above, while I was on the ground.

Our goal was to trick him into thinking that I was the only one chasing him, then have her jump down from above and pin him to the ground.

"Keiko!" she shouted.

The princess jumped down from the rooftops and landed at my side. Her brown leather boots were a few inches from my face. My mind went blank at the sight.

I glanced at the soles of her boots, only to work my way slowly upwards. I followed the edge of those crisp boots all the way to their tops. Behind the boots were two long thin pieces of fabric. I followed the fabric up her body with my eyes. The rich black color sparkled off the three suns' rays. My heartbeat started to echo through my ears. I could feel my face getting warmer as I followed them up even higher.

Eventually, the fabric faded away, and all that was left was skin. I could feel my eyes widen. *I had never really noticed it till now, but the princess has a beautiful pair of flawless legs.*

"Keiko…"

"Keiko…"

I was hearing a faint voice.

Is somebody calling my name? Eh, whatever. I'm too busy admiring these beautiful legs right now.

"Keiko!" the princess shouted and slapped my face.

Smack!

"Oweeeee! What the heck was that for?" I asked, rubbing my cheek.

"Is this really the time to be fantasizing? We need to go, he's getting away!"

"Oh crap! You're right, let's go," I said.

I put my hand in the princess's and pulled myself up from the ground. We began to run again, this time mixing up the plan.

Since the cloaked figure had just knocked me down with a crate, it was safe to assume that he thought I was out of the equation. If the princess showed up and started chasing him, she could lure him into an area where I could pounce on him from above. The plan should work out in our favor. After all, there was only one of him, and there were two of us.

I was now leaping across countless rooftops, trying to keep up with the princess. Predicting where she was going wasn't the hard part; the hard part was predicting the cloaked figure's movements.

The princess could run up behind him on the right side and shoot a combat spell at him with the expectation of him turning left, but that wouldn't necessarily be the case. The figure would occasionally leap over the spell and go right, or jump upward, kick off the wall and go back in the direction he'd come. It was making it quite difficult to follow along.

Even so, it was all going according to plan and the figure was nearing the ambush zone. I gave the princess the signal that I was ready.

Wait... wait... he's almost here.

I stood with my eyes locked on the target, just waiting for the perfect moment to make my attack.

And... now!

I leaped off the rooftop towards the alleyway, next to the four-story house that the figure was cornered up against. For once, I was about to do something right the first time.

I landed on top of the cloaked figure. I felt his legs buckle under my weight as he dropped to the floor. I quickly grabbed the vials and hid them back in my sash.

"Now... it's time to see who you are."

I reached for the hood of his cloak with anticipation. My arm shook and the smile on my face widened. I was finally able to understand why the royal guards loved doing what they did. This excitement, this anticipation. "I can't take it anymore!"

I grabbed the cloak and ripped it off the figure. The edges of his crisp white hair glistened in the light, complementing his vibrant green eyes. His skin was pale, but he was a little darker than the rest of us. His hair covered his ears and most of his face, leaving only a bit of it exposed.

"Oh... he's just a normal human." *But for him to wield jumping magic—that's a rare sight.*

"Keiko. That's not a human, that's an—"

Splat!

"Ahhh, my eyes!"

A black creamy liquid had been shot into my eyes. I could hear the princess screaming too. She must have also been attacked. I could feel the man breaking free from my grip. I rapidly wiped the goop out of my eyes. I then ran up to the princess and wiped it from hers too.

"Come here, princess. I'm not dealing with this any longer. I need a break!"

I grabbed the princess's shoulders and pulled her in towards me. Our lips locked. Just as I'd hoped, the tingling feeling in my chest appeared once more. I pushed her away and reached into the glowing light in the center of my chest.

What the? This doesn't feel like a sword or a spear.

I grabbed the cold handle of the weapon inside my chest and pulled outwards. "A bow? At a time like this?"

I was hoping for the spear or the chained sword so I could launch it at him, but I guess this would have to do.

"Ignite," I said.

A large water-vapor arrow formed right beside me. I put it on the bowstring and pulled back, and then I let fly.

The thin string rubbed the edges of my fingers as it was flung forwards. My eyes were locked onto the arrow. My pupils widened, allowing more sunlight to enter them, giving me the best view possible of the shot I was about to land. I saw the man turn his head back. The fear in his eyes was clearly visible.

"It's gonna hit!"

Splat!

"Wahhh!" I shouted.

Black goop had once again been shot directly onto my eyes.

Boom!

The arrow's explosion went off, meaning only one thing: the target had not been hit. "Noooooo! I missed it."

I fell to my knees. Tears of sadness washed away the goop on my face. The thrill I'd once felt was now gone.

"Keiko, get up!" the princess shouted. "There's another cloaked figure on that rooftop!"

She was right. I looked up towards the rooftop she was pointing at and saw a smaller figure. It was casting a spell that was launching the black goop in our direction. I looked back over towards the man. He was now unconscious on the ground; most likely from the blast. I still had possession of the vials, and that was all I cared about.

Now there's two of them? Why do they want the vials so badly? There's a whole dragon carcass hanging from the clock tower. Unless they don't necessarily want any dragon's blood—is it possible that they dont want us examining it?

"Show yourself!" I shouted to the cloaked figure on the rooftop.

There was a subtle breeze. The cloak on the figure was being caught in the wind. It was obvious that this figure was a woman, I could tell by the little bit of her legs that was being revealed by the cloak's movement.

A moment of silence went by, but shortly afterwards the woman ripped the cloak off her body. The princess and I stood there in shock. Her legs were gorgeous and slim. She was small and petite, and had long red hair that shimmered in the sunlight. Her crimson eyes were locked on to mine, but that wasn't what had shocked the princess and me. It was her ears.

The breeze blew her hair towards the left side of her face, exposing her right ear. It was like nothing I had ever seen before. The tip of it was pointed.

"Ahh, my head hurts," the man said as he got up off the ground.

I looked over at him. The breeze lifted his hair out of his face, revealing that he too had pointy ears.

The princess spoke: "I knew it. Keiko, go get them!"

The collar around my neck appeared from thin air, only to glow blue before vanishing again. My body started to move on its own.

"Woah! Ahhh!"

I was still new to this whole maid thing, and the collar wasn't helping. The princess's command had forced my body to move on its own; the power of the collar was truly remarkable. My legs bent down and shot up, causing me to leap into the air.

Woah! This collar has control over my magic abilities, too?

Up until now, I'd thought that the collar was only capable of controlling my physical abilities, but it seemed that I'd been wrong. While I was focused on the red haired girl, the princess went after the man.

"Hey, redhead! Why don't we make this easy? Surrender to me and I won't have to hurt you," I said with my best seductive smile.

"My name is not 'redhead,' it's Aoi! And I will do no such thing," the girl said.

Aoi? Doesn't that translate as blue? Ah, whatever, that's not the point!

A looked her dead in the eyes. I could tell that she was ready to put up a fight. Judging from her appearance, it was safe to assume that she wasn't from around here.

She had on a white shirt that she'd paired with a red leather jacket that was similar in style to the one I wore. Over her legs she wore a pair of leggings that ran all the way up her body. She also had on a white skirt that sat just above her leggings. Around her right leg there was a ribbon that matched the color of her jacket. She wore small black gloves on her hands and on her feet she sported a pair of little red shoes.

She looked so fragile and innocent, but I was wary of the incredibly powerful magic I could smell radiating from her body. The collar around my neck was not going to let me leave without bringing Aoi with me. The last thing I wanted to do was blow up this whole town after just having saved it. There was only one thing left that I could do... grovel!

I dropped to my knees and bent my face down towards the ground. "Please come with me. I beg of you!" I shouted.

"What the heck? Aren't you supposed to be some kind of warrior?" Aoi demanded.

I glanced up at her face. Much like her outfit, her face was now blazing red. She looked disgusted, yet rather flustered.

"Listen, Aoi. Can I call you that? Anyway, the princess has this slave collar around my neck, and if I don't do what she demands of me I'll be in for some serious trouble. Now, I haven't actually experienced what happens if I'm unable to complete a task, but I really don't want to find out. So how about we—"

"Hold up… a slave collar?" she said.

"Yeah, it's being hidden with illusion magic currently, but it's very much still there. Anyway, I would greatly appreciate it if you and your boyfriend could please simply come with us for some questioning."

Aoi took a few steps back in disgust. "Ewww! He's not my boyfriend, he's my brother! Why are we even having this conversation? You're supposed to be my enemy!" she shouted.

Her face was flushed and her body was trembling, but not from fear. Her smell had changed; I no longer sensed an immense amount of magic. *Has she let her guard down?*

I stood up from my hunched-over position and took a step closer to her. Her face was even more flushed and I could tell that she was anxious.

"Why are you so nervous?" I asked. *Wait... could it be?*

"Nervous? I am not nervous! Just because this is the first time I've come in contact with another man besides my immediate family does not mean that I am nervous!"

Aoi covered her mouth with both her hands. It was then that a thought popped into my head. *Oh, this is gonna be fun.*

Before I'd met the princess, whenever I wasn't stealing I was at the bar with my good friend Fujio. Fujio was the local drunk of the kingdom. It didn't matter which bar I walked into, he was always there. We spent our days smooth-talking women. Looking back, I think the only reason Fujio accepted me was because he didn't realize that I was a demihuman. He was always so drunk that he probably thought he was seeing things.

I took a couple steps closer to Aoi. Her small body was shaking with fear. I once again put on my best smile. Once I was close enough, I wrapped my arm around her shoulder and whispered in her ear. I could tell that my whispering was working.

"Aoi, what a beautiful name," I said.

She turned her eyes away from mine.

"Hey, why don't we get out of here and go somewhere else? I know a castle that happens to have an unoccupied room at the moment."

"Wha-what? N-n-no, I could never. Not with the enemy," she said, trembling.

Perfect! It's working. If I can just convince her that I'm a good guy and get her to come along with me, then I won't have to deal with the collar's punishment later!

"No? Don't you think that it'll be lots of fun?" I asked her.

Her face had begun to glow brighter than her hair. I had to admit that she did look beautiful. Her big eyes were adorable, and those pointy ears of hers were the cutest things I had ever seen.

"Well... maybe it would be fun," she said in a subtle voice.

It's working! Now all I have to do is hit her with the finisher.

"Well if that's the case, why don't we—"

Boink!

"Ahhhh! What was that?"

I turned around angrily. My mood shifted immediately when I saw that the princess was standing behind me. In her left hand she held Aoi's brother, who was still unconscious, and in her right hand was a large stick.

"Oh... princess! You see, I was just—"

Boink!

"Ahhhh! Hey, let me finish!"

"I've heard enough. Now take him, so I can deal with her."

The princess hurled the man's unconscious body into my arms. Aoi regained her senses and stood her ground against the princess.

"My name is Aoi, and I will not lose to you, princess!"

Boink!

The princess whacked Aoi on the head with her stick. As a result, Aoi too, fell unconscious.

"Princess! What an amazing job!" I said.

"Shut up! Pick them up and let's get back to the kingdom so Lola can analyze the dragon's blood. While we're at it, I have a few questions for these two," she said.

The princess looked angry. Her face was red and her hands were clenched into fists. I could see literal steam coming out of her body.

"Hey, princess, I was just trying to—"

"Shut up and sit!" she commanded.

My body jolted to the floor and I fell silent.

I've really gone and done it, haven't I?

Chapter 18
The Truth

Keiko and the princess made their way back to the kingdom. Upon arrival, they headed straight for Lola at the Adventurers' Guild.

The princess ordered me to carry both Aoi and her brother. My arms were screaming in protest. Carrying them hadn't seemed like such a hard task, but after ten hours of walking back to the kingdom my arms were ready to give out.

The princess slammed open the guild doors. The whole guild shifted their attention towards her, the room fell silent. She marched straight up to the front desk, and I followed close behind her. The silence of the guild members, paired with their judgmental stares, was sending chills down my spine.

Lola's eyes widened at the sight of us. She smiled widely and her cheeks lifted with joy.

"If it isn't Valentina herself. Oh, and I see wolf-boy is with you too!" she said. *Really... this crap again?*

"What's he doing with those two people?" Lola asked.

"Nevermind them. We have the vials of blood that you asked for," I said.

Lola rushed to my side and covered my mouth with her hands. It was clear that the princess was still angry. A dark aura was radiating off of her body, and Lola's hands on my face were not helping the situation.

"You have to be quiet, Keiko! It would be a bad thing if anybody heard you. This is a secret quest, after all," Lola said.

I mumbled into her hands. "My bad."

Lola escorted us to a room, away from the guild members' view. Once inside, I put the two siblings down and tied them up with some rope that Lola provided. As they were visible magic users, the rope was most likely not going to hold them for long, but it would stop them from casting any spells that required body movements.

From there we were escorted back to the vault. Going through that dark portal still gave me chills, but I did what I had to do. After entering the vault, I noticed that the map on the table was emitting three red lights.

I walked over to the table. On the map near the Lake of Wonders were three red Xs. I placed my fingers on the map, only to see a change shortly afterwards.

Lola and the princess walked up behind me. They also observed how the map changed. It started to bubble around the Lake of Wonders, almost like it was being boiled. The parchment burned away at the center of the bubbles. *Strange, there's no flame.*

The map burned for a few short seconds creating a decent-sized hole where the lake had been. We all stood there, watching. A few more seconds passed, and the map changed again—it began to recreate itself. The burnt pieces started to reform back onto the map's surface. We watched as the map pieced itself back together, revealing a new location. The lake was no longer there; it was now a large pool of lava, surrounded by purple stone and burnt forest.

"What the heck happened to the lake?" Lola shouted.

"It was Keiko's fault," said the princess.

"Huh? My fault? How is it at all my fault?"

The princess turned her head and crossed her arms. "Hmph!"

"Anyway, may I have the vials of dragon's blood, please?" Lola asked.

I gave her the vials after removing them from my sash. Lola

then used creation magic to form four new identical empty vials.

Creation magic is a low-grade type of magic. It allows the user to recreate a perfectly identical copy of an object in their hand. Some consider creation magic to be the most powerful magic around, while others consider it to be useless on the battlefield. Although creation magic doesn't require much of the user, I had never learned it. I was quite amazed to see it performed in person.

"Thanks, Lola," I said with a smile.

"No problem! It was nothing at all," she replied.

Lola explained that she was going to send the vials to the kingdom's secret laboratory to get them tested immediately. "Before we do that, let's get you paid," she said.

Lola raised her hand above the map and tapped on each of the three Xs on the table. As she did so, blue holographic boxes appeared above them. The boxes contained information about each type of creature and who had defeated them. It broke down their strength levels and their magical abilities.

I was ecstatic. This had been my first official quest for the kingdom, and I was ready to receive my reward.

The first one read:

Entity: Minotaur

Strength: K-D

Magic levels /1000: 15

Attack levels /1000: 453

Defense levels /1000: 485

Reward for completion: 90,000 yupps

Status: Dead

Quest completed by: Valentina Bowatani an Keiko Hiro

My jaw dropped to the floor. "Ninety-thousand yupps!" *That's more money than Grandpa and I ever stole in our entire lives!*

The second one read:

Entity: Headless Knight

Strength: K-DD

Magic levels /1000: 786

Attack levels /1000: 554

Defense levels /1000: 686

Reward for completion: 118,000 yupps

Status: Dead

Quest completed by: Valentina Bowatani and Keiko Hiro

The Third one read:

Entity: Crimson Dragon

Strength: K-DDD

Magic levels /1000: 1000

Attack levels /1000: 783

Defense levels /1000: 891

Reward for completion: 284,000 yupps

Status: Dead

Quest completed by: Valentina Bowatani and Keiko Hiro + Other(s)

Drool started to dribble down from my mouth. "Four hundred ninety-two thousand yupps!"

Lola giggled. "Mm-hmm. That's right! This is the type of reward you receive when completing secret quests for the kingdom."

I looked over at the princess. She seemed unfazed. It was hard to tell if she just wasn't that excited by the amount, or if she was holding back her feelings because she was mad at me. It was probably pocket change to her, but to me it was life-changing. The average salary in Zaria was one hundred twenty thousand yupps per year, and possibly a little more if you were lucky.

"Lola, there's something I'm a bit confused about," the princess said.

'What is it?" Lola asked.

"If the dragon was rated K-B in terms of strength, and it was a green quest, then what color rating did the minotaur and headless knight have?"

She had a good point. It hadn't occurred to me that the dragon was only a mere green quest on the color scale for secret quests.

"Since the minotaur and headless knight were ranked lower, they shouldn't even be on the kingdom's secret quest list. How is that possible?" I asked.

Lola began to wave her hands frantically. "No, no. You have it all wrong. I guess I should have explained this to you guys earlier! The kingdom's secret quests have a different ranking system then the normal quests. Since these quests deal with highly dangerous and unknown creatures, we use a bigger, more in-depth ranking system."

Lola went on to explain the ranking system for the kingdom's top secret quests. According to her, they were ranked like so:

Green Quest: Easy

Ranking: K-D - K-DDD

Yellow Quest: Slightly Harder

Ranking: K-C - K-CCC

Purple Quest: Hard

Ranking: K-B - K-BBB

Red Quest: Hardest

Ranking: K-A - K-AAA

"The difficulty of the quest is determined by factors other than the creature's stats. Things such as the type of creature, their fighting style, the weapons they hold, and their previous track record with other adventurers come into account too," Lola said.

I stood there in confusion, and I could tell that the princess was feeling the same way.

"If that's the case, then how come a dragon was ranked in the green class? They have supposedly been extinct for years and the dragon's power was extraordinary," said the princess.

Lola smiled. "Well, princess, as much as I would love to give you a detailed response as to why it was such a low ranking, I can't. The map uses its magic to determine the ranking of all the creatures in the land of Geatree, and that is something I don't have any control over."

I glanced at the princess. She looked confused, but at the same time content with the answer that Lola had provided.

"Last question, Lola. I thought visible magic users were supposed to be rare and hard to find, that it was something that only a select few could use, but at the village where we defeated the dragon there were quite a few. Now, I don't mean to say that they were all powerful, as most of them could only use basic spells, but how is that possible?" I asked.

Lola sighed. "That's what we're trying to figure out. The kingdom believes that the dragon's blood might be the key to answering these questions."

I wish they would have told me that at the beginning. I had some dragon's blood on me!

Shortly afterwards, Lola escorted us back to the room in the guild where we had left the two siblings. She then set off to deliver the blood samples to the laboratory.

The princess commanded me to carry the siblings back to the castle. She said nothing else. Our walk was quiet; she didn't speak a single word to me. I tried to ease the tension with a few jokes, but they didn't land.

"I don't understand what I did wrong—I was just trying to convince Aoi to come along with us, and I figured the best way to do so was with seduction. It was clear that she had never seen a stranger male before, so I figured I would take advantage of that fact. That's all! I swear, princess! That's all that happened."

The princess stopped walking. The trees planted next to the pathway released tiny leaves that blew past our faces in the wind.

"Is that the truth?" she asked.

It was hard to see, since she was facing the other way, but judging from the color of her ears, it was safe to assume that her whole face was red.

"Yes, princess! I swear it's the truth," I said.

She turned in my direction, locking her eyes with mine. She marched over to me and grabbed the chain of my necklace. I could feel sweat forming on my face. I was nervous and shaken by her actions. I stood there quietly, looking into her eyes. I couldn't tell what she was about to do.

What if she commands me to do something painful or embarrassing? I wouldn't be surprised with the way she's been acting.

"Mhm!" *What is this?*

There was a soft sensation on my lips. It was the princess. Her lips were locked onto mine.

But… why? We're not fighting an enemy. Could it be that…

The princess broke contact with my lips. She placed her hands on my chest and looked towards the ground.

"Next time, find a different way to persuade her," she said.

Her face was flushed and she looked cuter than ever. Her hands felt so gentle and her hair looked so beautiful. My heart started to flutter.

"Yeah… I'll make sure to do that next time." I said.

After that, we made our way towards the castle again. The princess was more talkative, and seemed to be in a better mood.

So all it took was a kiss, huh?

Once we arrived at the castle, the princess had two royal knights escort us to the dungeon. The staircase was long and spiraled downwards. It was dark, and there were barely any torches on the walls. I felt uneasy. It wasn't long before I started to feel depressed. *This is where they must have kept Grandpa.*

I'd never told the princess about my grandfather. If I had, maybe she wouldn't have brought me to this place. Eventually we made it to the end of the staircase, and entered the dungeon.

It was dark and cold. We were so deep underground that the only source of light was through tiny cracks in the stone on the ceiling.

I handed the two siblings off to one of the royal guards. He sat the brother upright in a wooden chair in the center of one of the musty rooms. Then he took Aoi and tied a rope to the existing one around her body, hanging her from the ceiling. The princess glanced over at me.

"It's time to get some answers," she said.

Chapter 19
Answers

I walked up to Aoi's brother. The guard had made sure to tie him down to the chair so that he couldn't move. I looked at the ropes around his arms and legs; they looked tight and painful. I felt pity for the man.

Aoi's brother. I wonder what kind of man he is?

I brushed his long hair back with the idea of revealing his ears. I gasped at what I saw. The top half of his ears had been chopped off with some sort of blade. I knew all too well about that kind of thing.

"Awaken!" the princess shouted while splashing the siblings with cold water.

"Ahhhhh!" they shouted, waking from their slumber.

I felt uneasy. Aoi and her brother started to panic as they awoke.

"Where are we?" the brother exclaimed.

"Let me down this instant and untie me!" Aoi shouted.

"Enough!" the princess yelled.

The room went silent almost instantly. The princess might have looked all innocent and pure, but she could turn a room from warm to cold with a single word.

"Listen up, this is how it's going to go. I'm going to ask you both some questions, and you're going to answer them truthfully," the princess said.

"Why should we listen to a damn thing you say?" Aoi asked.

The princess looked annoyed, but confident in her response. "If you do as I say then you'll be set free after our conversation. If you don't cooperate then your brother sitting in the chair over there is going to be in for a world of pain."

My eyes widened in disbelief. She had to be joking. There was no way that the princess, the woman who'd risked her life countless times yesterday to save people she didn't even know, would torture a man just for some answers. Sweat beaded on the siblings' faces. Aoi's brother spoke to her.

"Aoi, just do as she says. Please, I can't take any more pain."

The look in Aoi's eyes was one of familiarity. I knew the feeling of watching someone you cared about get hurt because of you. Aoi nodded her head and agreed to follow the princess's instructions.

"First, both of you tell me your names."

The siblings were shocked. "You want to know our names?" the brother asked.

"That's what I said."

"My name is Umi," the brother answered.

"And my name is Aoi."

The princess responded to the siblings by introducing both of us by name.

"Now that that's out of the way, I have some other questions. Tell me, are you two human?"

"What would make you ask such a silly question?" Umi asked, laughing nervously.

His voice was choppy and he was obviously stuttering. It was clear that he was hiding something.

"Answer the question," the princess demanded.

Umi locked eyes with his sister. They looked frightened to answer.

"No... we're not humans," Aoi said.

So does that mean the princess and I were correct in our assumption?

"I thought so. So tell me, what race are you members of?" the princess asked.

"I... I can't say," Aoi said.

"Fair enough," said the princess.

The siblings exhaled in relief. As they did so, the princess walked over to Umi and pulled out her dagger. Umi looked up at the princess in fear.

"Wh-what's that for?"

"The rules were simple, were they not? You do as I say and you won't get hurt. Refuse to answer—and you do."

The princess slammed her dagger down through the fingers on Umi's right hand and into the arm of the wooden chair.

"Ahhhhhhhh!"

Umi's fingers began to bleed all over the arm of the chair and onto the floor. I couldn't believe what was happening. *Is this… the true nature of the princess?*

Aoi started to cry out to the princess: "I'm sorry—I'm sorry. I swear I'll talk, just stop. Please!"

Tears were running down their faces. I'd had no idea that the princess was capable of doing such a thing. My chest felt tight, and my heart was aching for Umi.

"So answer me, then!" the princess shouted.

"We… we…"

'You're what?" the princess asked.

"We're elves, damn it!" Aoi said.

I knew it. So we were correct.

The princess smiled. "Next question."

"Huh?" Aoi looked up from the ground. Tears were rolling down her cheeks and onto the floor.

"Hey, princess. Don't you think that you're being a little harsh?" I said.

"People who interfere with kingdom duties deserve no mercy," she said.

Has she always had this side to her? I can't believe it, I just can't!

"As I was saying, why did you try to steal the vials of blood from us earlier?"

"We were commanded to by our father," Umi replied.

"Oh? And how did he know what we were up to?" the princess asked.

"We had some scouts in the area. They alerted the kingdom that the crimson dragon had awoken, and that two beings were fighting it. Shortly afterwards, Father sent us to make sure no one was planning on tampering with it," Umi said.

The princess smiled. "Good answer, but I need more details."

She bent down in front of Umi and rested the blade of her dagger under his chin. She then lifted it until their eyes met.

"And what was the reason why your father did not want anyone tampering with the dragon?"

Umi gulped. "I... I... I can't—"

"Umi stop!" Aoi shouted. "I don't want you to die over some stupid secret. I'll tell her."

The princess walked over to Aoi. "Oh?"

I looked at Aoi from a distance. Her eyes were full of tears and she was trembling with fear. The princess was something else; she was a beast in disguise.

"It's because of the blood," Aoi said.

"What about it?" the princess asked.

"As I'm sure you know, dragons are creatures that have been created by the goblins and the elves, and which were granted magic powers and peace from the tree of life and blessed by the gods of this world."

"Yes, I am aware," the princess said.

I looked over at Aoi in confusion. "What does that have to do with anything?" I asked.

"I'm sure you figured this out already, but dragon's blood obviously has powerful magic from different lifeforms flowing through it. Tell me, princess, what do you think happens when a lower lifeform drinks that blood?"

"I... I don't know. What happens?" the princess asked.

"They die," Umi replied.

The room went silent. Sweat dripped down my face. I could feel my body temperature rising. *What does he mean, they die? I drank the blood!*

"Well .. yes. Umi is correct, but there's more to it than that. Didn't you find it strange that there were so many people capable of using visible magic in the village?"

"Yeah! I did find it strange," I said.

The princess agreed.

"That's because drinking dragon's blood allows the average human to use visible magic," Aoi said.

"What? Is that true?" I asked.

"Why would she lie?" Umi said.

"Isn't gaining the ability to use visible magic a good thing?

What about it makes them die?" I asked.

Aoi went on to explain the trouble caused by drinking dragon's blood. According to her, the first time a person drinks the blood their senses are heightened and they gain the ability to use low-class spells of visible magic. The problem is that the dragons' souls had been corrupted by the goblins before their final trans-formation, so all of that dark magic was still swarming in their blood. When a person drank the blood for the first time, they got a craving for more. The person with the craving then went on to drink even more blood, resulting in a power increase. What that person didn't know was that every time they drank the blood their soul got more corrupted. Eventually, the dark magic would take over completely and destroy their soul, leaving them dead. Luckily for me, I had only drunk it one time.

Strange. She's said all this, yet I've never felt a need to drink more blood, even when we were covered in it. Could it have been because I already had the use of visible magic?

"That all makes perfect sense, but there is still one thing I just don't understand. If it's true, then how did a handful of villagers get a hold of it in the first place?"

Umi gulped then began to speak: "The truth is… the elves gave it to them."

I couldn't believe what I was hearing. *The elves gave the humans dragon's blood to drink!*

"This is all so confusing. I have a couple of questions of my own if you don't mind me taking over here, princess?" I said.

"I have no problem with that," she answered.

"First off, this whole elf business is driving me insane. I thought the elves were eradicated centuries ago in the great war? So how are you even here?" I asked.

Umi went on to explain the truth behind the great war. According to him, after the creation of the beasts we called dragons had been a success, the elves and goblins had started to fight over who had control of them. The goblins felt responsible for creating the dragons, and thought they should have full control, and the elves felt the same way in turn.

Apparently, the goblins had gotten so fed up with the elves that they'd gone and made their own form of dragon behind their backs—a smaller and less powerful version which they called wyverns.

Wyverns were easy to produce, since they didn't use humans as their main subject. The goblins had sacrificed themselves for the creation of the wyvern. They'd used their weak and dying citizens, and given them new life through experimentation. They then launched a surprise attack on the elven kingdom when they were least expecting it.

The goblins had attacked riding wyverns. They slaughtered every last elf they could get their hands on; most of the total population alive at the time.

"Most of the men were killed in battle, and had their bodies sacrificed to the great dragon Larx in exchange for a blessing of the gods' power. But after centuries of selective breeding, we elves were able to replenish our population. The only problem is that an elf gives birth to a boy once out of every one-thousand babies," Umi said.

So that's why Aoi hasn't seen any men besides the ones in her immediate family. They're too busy being forced to breed with selected females!

"This is a lot to take in." I said. "Last and final question: why did you give the humans of that village dragon's blood?"

"Isn't that obvious? To trick them into killing each other," Umi said.

"How dare you?" the princess shouted.

She raised her dagger above Umi's leg and pushed it downwards. The tip of the dagger penetrated his upper thigh. Screams of agony filled the dungeon.

"Princess! That's enough. This wasn't part of the deal," I said.

The princess glanced at me; the sight of my face seemed to calm her down slightly. She removed the dagger from Umi's leg and walked over to Aoi, who was now crying even more after her brother's leg had been stabbed.

"Why did you do it, Aoi? Why?" she shouted.

Aoi's face was swimming with tears, making it hard for her to speak. "We were commanded to. We had no choice."

"Who commanded you to do it?" I asked.

"Our father—the King," she said.

Umi stopped his screaming and started to speak: "Please don't hurt her. Just listen to what I have to say."

I agreed that we would listen, on the princess's behalf. Umi went on to explain how the king of the elves had ordered them to kill the humans. He said that their father's goal was to have the humans go insane with power and kill each other.

By doing so he had hoped that it would create an opening for the goblins to come out of hiding and attack the human village, with the goal of taking it over. Then the elves could charge in and get revenge on the goblins for what they had done.

"Humans are not our real enemies. We have realized that the great war was a trivial matter, but the goblins, those backstabbing losers can never be forgiven!" Aoi shouted.

This was a lot to take in. Looking at Aoi's teary eyes, and Umi's bloody hand and thigh, made me once again pity the siblings. I knew this feeling too well.

"Princess, I think we've heard enough. Let's let them go," I said.

"Agreed. That's all I needed to hear," she said.

I got down on my knees and placed my hands on the floor. I looked up at the princess and begged her to use her magic to heal Umi's injuries.

"I know what they did was wrong, but they had no choice, princess. Please heal his fingers and his thigh!" I said.

Aoi's face was again red. I could see her eyelids quivering. Umi looked up at the princess, hoping she would agree.

"No, I won't be healing his fingers," she said.

"But princess—"

"Because this is all an illusion," she said.

The princess snapped her fingers. As she did so, a bright yellow aura radiated off her body and out through the room. The dungeon walls shifted from dark to light. Windows appeared on the walls and carpets on the floor. The room was now bright and full of sunshine, and the atmosphere had turned from cold to warm.

The scenery wasn't the only thing that changed. Umi's fingers reappeared on his hand as if they had never been cut off, and his thigh was flawless, as if it had never been stabbed.

We were no longer in the dungeon. We were now in the great hall.

"What's going on?" Aoi asked.

The princess smiled. "I would never go so low as to torture someone for answers, but with illusion magic I can torture them without actually doing so," she said.

My face lit up with joy and I felt more at ease.

I knew it. I knew it was all fake.

The king and his royal guards had been listening to our conversation the whole time.

"Well, Father, what do you think?"

King Bowatani got up from his throne and walked over to the siblings. He looked Umi in the face and asked him if what he said was true. Umi and Aoi insisted that they were telling the truth.

"Hmmm. I'll let them go on one condition," he said.

The two listened eagerly to what he had to say.

"When the time comes, I want you two to escort my daughter

and her maid to Lindia, the elven kingdom."

The two accepted his terms. Soon afterwards, they were released from their bindings and set free. Just before they left, Aoi approached me. Her face was red, and she was stammering.

"Th-thanks for standing up to the princess for me and my brother..."

She handed me a small flute about half a handspan in length.

"If you ever need my help, just blow on this whistle and I'll come as quickly as I can."

Before I could thank her, Aoi took off running to her brother's side. The two elves darted out of the palace and back towards their own kingdom.

"What was that?" the princess asked.

"Oh, nothing!" I said, shoving the flute deep into the pouch on my sash.

I looked at the princess. She didn't seem too upset. She actually looked tired.

"Well, I'm glad this is all over, princess."

"Not exactly. We left a whole dragon carcass at the village," she said.

Oh crap! I forgot about that. We did, didn't we?

"I guess we gotta go back, huh?" I said.

The princess sighed. "Yeah, we do."

Cough, cough!

"Go back where, exactly?" the King asked.

The princess's face was suddenly full of fear. She started to tremble and her voice cracked.

"I thought you said the royal guards caught the elves. What's this about you going back?" he asked.

The princess struggled to speak. It was clear that her father was still unaware that she had unsealed her true powers. *I have to help her.*

"It was me!" I shouted. "I forced the princess to go to the village. I couldn't stand to see that village destroyed by the dragon, so I made the princess come with me. I gave it my all, sir, and your daughter was nothing short of supportive."

I stood there nervously. *I hope he buys it!*

He looked at me in silence for what felt like an eternity. The tension in the room was high. *What's going to happen?*

"Okay, if you say so," he said.

The princess and I let out a massive sigh of relief. She looked over at me and smiled. I could tell that she was grateful.

"By the way, Valentina, what's with that outfit?" he asked.

"Uhh… it's my interrogation uniform!" she said nervously.

"Hmm… Okay."

The princess and I let out another massive sigh of relief. The princess looked at me and we both began to laugh. Her laugh was beautiful; truly music to my ears.

"Hey, Keiko."

"What is it, princess?" I asked.

"Meet me in my room in five minutes," she said

My eyes widened and I felt my face heating up. The princess smiled and made her way out of the hall and up to her room.

Did I hear her correctly? Did she say her room?

After a five-minute wait, a royal maid of the king's household escorted me to her room. I followed her up a long spiral staircase and down a dimly lit hallway. As we walked, the maid began to ramble on about the princess.

"God! I still can't believe that the princess chose you, of all people, to be her personal maid. Not only that, but it seems that for some reason, you are exempt from wearing the required uniform," she said.

I followed her in silence. After all, she was right.

I began to ponder. *Why was it that the princess chose me, and why doesn't she enforce the dress code on me?*

I began to ask myself so many questions, but I kept my mouth shut. It was already enough that I was being forced to be a maid to the daughter of the man who'd executed my grandfather, and the last thing I wanted to do was upset his personal maid. If I caused trouble now, who knew what would happen to me.

Eventually, we arrived at the princess's room. "Here we are," said the maid, pointing to the wooden door. "Don't be too frisky, now."

"Please," I said, and rolled my eyes.

Do I knock or...?

I reached for the door handle with my right hand. I turned it and slowly pushed open the squeaky door. I entered the room and as I did so I happened to notice how girly it was. I had never been in a girl's room before, but I couldn't say that I was surprised.

I took a moment to admire all of the expensive jewelry that was just lying around. I picked up one of the jewels and held it close to my eye. This single jewel would have been enough to release me and Grandpa Mist from the grip of poverty, and she had dozens of them. I put the jewel down and wandered around the room.

"Princess? Are you here?" I asked.

Hmm! No response. Where could she be?

I heard the sound of flowing water coming from beyond a wooden door in the corner of her room. *Oh? She must be in the shower.*

"Ahhhhh!"

Crash!

What the…?

I swung the door open at the sound of the princess screaming.

"Princess! Are you okay?" I shouted, bursting in.

I looked down at the floor, only to find that the princess was lying there naked from head to toe, with a bucket of water on top of her head. Our eyes locked. Both of our faces began to turn beet red.

Within seconds, an aura of darkness covered her. Even so, in that moment nothing could have distracted me from the pain of her slap on my left cheek.

"Ahhhhh!" she shouted. "Keiko, get out!" She tossed the wooden bucket at me.

I darted out of the bathroom and back into her bedroom. My breathing was fast and my heart was racing like crazy. This girl was scarier than any of the magical beasts we had taken on so far. I started to reflect on what I had just seen. The thought of the princess's damp, glistening skin made my body feel oddly warm.

Am I embarrassed for her? I asked myself.

After I'd spent a few minutes patiently waiting for the princess to come out, she did. She had a towel on her head, wrapped around her hair, and a short purple bathrobe covering up her bare skin.

The sight of her long bare legs poking out the bottom of her robe was exhilarating. She looked over at me with a face that was clearly flustered. She was unable to look me in the eyes.

"What is it?" she asked.

I was shocked. I had never seen the princess in this state before. *Who is this person?*

"Well, you did call me here, princess. Sorry if I intruded." I said.

She walked over to her giant bed and sat down. She crossed one leg over the other and coughed into her closed fist.

"Right, that's correct," she said.

Almost instantly, her cute complexion was gone, and she was

right back to being her cool and collected self. She glanced up in my direction.

"Sit," she said.

Oh come on!

The collar around my neck activated and my body fell to the floor. As I sat down, I couldn't help but wonder what the princess wanted to discuss with me.

"We need to gather more information on the mythical creatures that have been appearing in Zaria, as well as dig up some more information on the elves."

I glanced up at her. "Speaking of that, aren't you shocked? I mean, we just found out that the elves are still alive, and that another major war could potentially happen in the future!" I said.

The princess nodded in agreement. She, too, saw this as a major problem. "Well, it seems to me that this Aoi girl has taken a liking to you. She could be a potential ally if we're able to persuade her to help us."

Why is her face turning red? I wondered.

I nodded in agreement. I felt that Aoi could be a potential ally, too. We talked for about a half hour on what our next steps should be. We came to the conclusion that even though we now knew about Lindia, that we wouldn't pursue it any further until we had some more information.

There was a reason that the dragon had been there. After all, just a few years before that lake had been empty, you could see straight to the bottom with ease. We decided that the best thing to do was to go back to the village and clean up all of the dragon's blood, and confiscate any bottles of it that the people had collected. The last thing we wanted was for the power of visible magic to get into the wrong hands.

After our long talk, the princess looked up at me. "You did good today, Keiko," she said. "I was unaware that there were other people who could keep up with my magical abilities. Even though you were tired and on the brink of death multiple times, you stayed by my side and helped me fight. For that, I give you my greatest thanks."

The princess placed her hand on top of my head and rubbed it. Normally I wasn't one to like head rubs. They made me feel like a useless dog—but this one I thoroughly enjoyed.

A small tear welled up in my left eye, only to trail down my cheek. The princess stopped petting me.

"What's wrong, Keiko?" she asked.

I sat there in shock. *What is this? Am I crying?*

I looked up at the princess. It was the first time anyone had ever treated me like a normal human, and not like trash because of my demihuman blood. I smiled.

"Thank you, princess. I mean it," I said.

She smiled, too. "Let's get some rest. We have a long day ahead of us tomorrow," she said.

"Yeah, let's do that. Hey… by the way, where must I sleep?" I asked. "It's just that, I only see one bed, and according to the long list of rules one of the other servants made me read earlier, a personal maid is not supposed to leave their master's side."

The princess's eyes widened in realization. My guess was that she had forgotten all about that rule. She looked down at her bed, while slightly gripping her sheets in her hands.

"I guess you can sleep here, but just for tonight!" she said.

I looked at the princess's flustered face and laughed. She looked adorable.

"What is it?" she asked.

"It's nothing," I said.

I hopped into bed beside the princess. The lights turned off and her room went dark. I was lying on my back, staring at the ceiling.

Thank you, princess, for believing in me. I won't let you down.

To be continued...

SPECIAL THANKS TO THE FOLLOWING PEOPLE FOR HELPING TO BRING THIS NOVEL TO LIFE

Eli Horowitz
Richard Yu
James Haynes
James Rowland Jr.
Kathleen Hanegraaf
Eric Estrada

Made in the USA
Middletown, DE
03 March 2023